Highlander Untamed

by

Cynthia Breeding

Ghosts of Culloden, Book 2

Highlander Untamed

Cover Art by *The Wild Rose Press, Inc.*

The Wild Rose Press, Inc.
PO Box 708
Adams Basin, NY 14410-0708
Visit us at www.thewildrosepress.com

Publishing History
First Edition, 2024
Trade Paperback ISBN 978-1-5092-5553-5
Digital ISBN 978-1-5092-5554-2

Ghosts of Culloden, Book 2
Published in the United States of America

Foreword

The Scottish New Year's Eve festival of "Hogmanay" has its roots in ancient Celtic and Norse lore. Sturdy sticks (hogmanaies) up to ten feet in length were wrapped in animal hide, ignited, and paraded around the town square at midnight. The smoke was believed to ward off evil for the coming year. The torches were then thrown into a river and the townspeople would gather in a large circle dance which often ended in embracing couples hieing to the nearest place of privacy.

Another tradition was that of "first-footing," which meant the first person to set foot in another person's home after midnight with a gift—usually whisky—would bring good luck to the inhabitants. Highland hospitality always welcomed strangers and, in the case of first-footing, preferably dark-haired men (who were the antidote to the blond, marauding Viking invaders of auld) would be the first-footers and thus offer protection to the family within.

And so the legend of dark-haired male strangers begins…

Prologue

New Year's Eve, Present Day
Inverness, Scotland

Vihansa Sutherland looked along the crowded street on the banks of the River Ness. It was nearing midnight, and men, most wearing traditional kilts, were lighting the hogmanay torches they would carry while they circled the base of the castle cliff.

"This is so much better than watching the ball drop in Times Square!" Thea—short for Athena—one of Vi's lifelong friends from Dallas, said as the men marched off.

"Probably because we've all only watched it on TV," Vi replied.

"I wouldn't want to be crushed in that New York City crowd anyway," Thea answered. "This is so much more manageable."

"Quite a lot of masculinity on view tonight, wouldn't you say?" Charlotte, another childhood friend along for their vacation, giggled. "Maybe we'll all find our Mr. Rights tonight."

Vi refrained from rolling her eyes. Charlotte was a romance writer and tended to use her overly active imagination to see romantic possibilities in any situation. "I'm not looking for 'Mr. Right.' I'm here to gather material for the paper I'm going to present to the history department at TU when we get back."

"On eighteenth century war weapons." Charlotte looked heavenward. "Why you ever picked such a topic when you could delve into real Scottish history with all its wondrous legends, I'll never understand."

"Filled with romantic heroes, no doubt." Vi smiled to soften the remark. "I chose weaponry precisely *because* it's not a topic women should care about. At least, not in the esteemed ranks of male faculty with tenure. My mother did name me after a Germanic war goddess, after all. Besides," she shrugged, "I've always wanted to walk the Culloden battlefield and re-imagine the battle."

"That the Scots lost," Thea said. "Isn't that kind of depressing?"

"Maybe, but they were fighting for something they believed in," Vi answered. "And they could have won if the strategy had been better planned."

"Well, there's not much we can do about that, over two hundred years later," Thea said. "I hope I don't have a bad reaction when we go."

Vi didn't reply immediately. Even as kids, Thea had always had an uncanny empathy for people in distress, which was why she owned an "alternative science" shop dedicated to self-healing with its use of herbs, crystals, and other things formerly considered New Age.

"Oh, look!" Charlotte interrupted the silence. "The men are coming back."

Vi squinted at the array of bobbing lit torches approaching the river bank. "Why are only men carrying the torches?" she asked. "That's a bit medieval, isn't it?"

"Ye doona expect the womenfolk to do it, do ye, lassie?"

Vi managed—just barely—not to jump out of her skin at the sound of the man's voice behind her. Her friends were staring over her shoulder, both nearly gaping.

Slowly, she turned. And managed—just barely—not to inhale sharply.

The man—he actually looked like a warrior, since he was wielding a sword that looked very real. His muscular arms were bare and he wore only a leather vest across his broad chest. His long black hair was in disarray and his eyes blazed like blue fire. Somehow, she managed to find her voice.

"Are you an enactor?"

"A what?"

Vi pointed. "Have you been hired to act out a scene with that?"

He looked down at the sword, a puzzled look on his face. "Act?" He scowled suddenly and sheathed the weapon so quickly it was only a blur of metal. "Nae." His expression changed as he looked her up and down. "Ye are a fine-looking lassie, ye are."

It was Vi's turn to scowl. She might be wearing an eighteenth-century costume, but this was the twenty-first century and the guy was acting chauvinistic. "I am not a lassie."

One eyebrow quirked. "Nae? Then what would ye be if ye are nae a lass?"

He seemed to genuinely want an answer. She felt Charlotte's not-so-gentle elbow nudge to her back and cleared her throat. "I am a...lady. I just don't like—"

"Ye are highborn, then?"

She furrowed her brow for a minute. "No. No, I didn't mean that I'm an aristocrat or anything—"

3

"They're starting the circle dance!" Charlotte interrupted.

"And it's being led by a lady with long, auburn hair," Thea said. "Maybe not so medieval after all?"

The man laughed. Vi grimaced.

Charlotte grabbed Thea's hand and looked at Vi. "Let's go."

Vi waved them on and turned back to the stranger to finish her thought. "I meant to say, I'm just a person. Vihansa is my name."

A corner of his mouth lifted. "Well, then, Vihansa. Would ye do me the honor of joining the dance?"

She hadn't planned to dance at all, but maybe she should cave this time. She had sort of overreacted to him calling her a lassie. Giving him a small smile, she nodded. "I would like that."

He grinned and took her hand. She could feel the rough callous of his fingertips, which probably meant he actually used that sword. Although his touch was gentle, she could also feel the strength in his hand. She wondered what line of work he was in.

Maybe, after the dance, he'd let her take a closer look at the weapon itself.

He tucked her hand inside his arm and, as he did so, her fingers grazed the hilt of the sword, and for a moment she felt a sharp tingle.

And then the world turned hazy and white.

Chapter One

New Year's Eve, 1745
Inverness, Scotland

Vi blinked her eyes several times as the strange white mist that had suddenly enveloped the festivities began to dissipate. She had heard of hoar fog but wasn't sure that was what this was. Or had been. It was gone now.

So were the city lights. Only a few torches left burning on posts and the moon casting a silvery glow on the river illuminated the area. Had there been an electrical outage? She squinted, trying to see into the darkness beyond. She couldn't see the building down the street and, across the river, the Best Western seemed to have disappeared too. For a moment, she wondered if Brigadoon had descended, then gave herself an inward shake. She was beginning to think like Charlotte.

Next to her, the tall Scot she'd almost danced with suddenly grinned. "Well, lassie. Seems the party is over."

Lassie. Hadn't she told him not to call her that? She was about to remind him, when she was practically pushed aside by two young women who both sidled up to him.

"Och, Robbie," one of them said in a seductive voice, "I'd been looking forward to dancin' with ye."

"So had I," the other one said, sounding more petulant as she gave Vi a dark look before turning her attention back. "All the other girls danced with ye this eve."

"Doona fash, lasses." He favored each of them with a charming smile. "There'll be another ceilidh in a fortnight or so. I promise ye will have the first two dances."

Both of the women giggled their assent, the one running her hand up his arm while the other brushed his chest before they both left.

Vi could hardly believe her eyes or ears. Those women had practically thrown themselves at him and he acted like it was his due. He certainly hadn't seemed to mind their rubbing all over him, either. She practically snorted. The man—Robbie—was a modern-day Lothario, just like her ex, Matt, had been.

Or—maybe—*modern-day* wasn't the right term to use. Vi's nape began to prickle as she looked around. The environment had changed. Now that her sight was more accustomed to the dark, she could see the dispersing crowd moving toward horses and buggies, not cars. There was no sign of modernization anywhere. Even the cathedral just down the street was no longer there. And where were Thea and Charlotte?

She squelched a brief bubble of hysteria that threatened to erupt. She was not the panicky sort. There had to be a logical explanation. She just didn't know what it was. Yet.

Then a thought struck her. The sword. She remembered she'd felt a tingle when her fingers touched it just before she'd been lost in the mist. Vi glanced down to where the hilt protruded from the leather sheath. It was ordinary-looking. No gold or silver trim and certainly not jewel-encrusted. She chided herself silently. She wasn't looking for Excalibur. Leave that kind of nonsense to Charlotte. She had thought maybe it was a ceremonial sword of sorts, since he was wearing it at a traditional dance. She didn't believe in "magic" or even rituals— leave that stuff to Athena—but she'd had some kind of reaction to touching the weapon.

"Ye've been looking a wee bit long at a certain part of me." A corner of Robbie's mouth quirked up. "Is there something ye'd be wanting?"

Vi felt her face flush as she shifted her gaze to his face. She couldn't even pretend to be indignant over the subtle innuendo, given where she'd been staring. He had no idea she'd been looking at the sword hilt instead of his sporran or—in his mind—what was *under* the sporran.

"I'd like to see your weapon."

His eyebrows nearly took flight and she realized that the words had come out wrong. *Really* wrong. "I...I...mean...your sword." God, was that any better? She never fumbled for words. She pointed before he could make a remark. "*That* one."

He looked down and then back to her. "Ye wouldna be wanting to run me through with it, would ye?"

"Of course not. I just..." Was she still fumbling for words? "I...was taught to admire good workmanship, and the hilt looks well made." That much was true at least. She had studied weaponry.

He gave her a dubious look but slowly pulled out the sword and held it in front of him, tip pointing up. "If ye doona mind, I'll hold on to it."

It was a reasonable statement, given that he was

probably wondering just how sane she was for asking to see a sword. Obviously, he wasn't going to let her take it. "Of course. May I touch it?"

He gave her another doubtful look. "Which part, lass?"

Did he think she wanted to test the razor-sharp edges? She bit back that retort. He probably already thought she was loony. "Just the hilt. It looks so smooth."

He adjusted his hold so his palms cradled the sword by its cross-guard, leaving the hilt free. Even so, as she ran her fingers over it, she brushed his hands. An unfamiliar tingle shot through her arm. Not *the* tingle, just *a* tingle.

She stepped back and looked around. She was still here. Wherever *here* was.

"Thank you. It seems to be a remarkable piece."

"'Twas my grandfather's." He sheathed the weapon. "I've nae seen ye around these parts. I'm sure I would have noticed." Robbie gave her the same infectious smile he'd used on the other women.

She was not about to be taken in with that smile. Matt had had a charming one too. But there wasn't any sense in making that obvious right now since she had no idea what was going on. At least he hadn't asked why she was so interested in a sword.

"I'm…visiting."

"And do ye have a name?"

Hadn't she already told him that? Lord, if he couldn't even remember her name after just a few minutes… She sighed. "Vihansa."

"'Tis unusual. I've nae heard it before."

So he hadn't remembered her name. Typical of charming men.

"What does it mean?" Robbie tilted his head and smiled at her. "Your name?"

At least he was curious. She gave him a direct look. "It's of Germanic origin. My mother studied abroad and became interested in their deities."

"Deities?"

She took a deep breath. He was probably going to laugh. "Vihansa was a goddess of warriors."

His smile widened into a grin. 'I can see how the goddess part suits ye."

He was flirting? She might be flattered—he *was* a virile, good-looking male, she couldn't deny that—but she'd been conned before. "I am more intrigued that medieval people put a female goddess in charge of soldiers."

Instead of making some sort of chauvinistic remark like she'd expected, he simply nodded. "I've got a cousin who'd agreed with ye. She wishes she could join the Cause."

She was beginning to have an inkling into what the "Cause" was, but it might be better if she didn't ask for clarification. "Maybe men should remember that Boudicca led the Incenis against the Romans." She stopped short of saying there was a bronze statue of her in London near the Westminster Bridge. If her "inkling" was correct, the statue hadn't been built yet. "She was successful."

"Aye. My cousin is fond of that story." He looked around at the nearly empty streets. "May I escort ye somewhere, Vihansa? I hope ye doona mind me using your Christian name since I doona ken your other."

"Sutherland. My last name is Sutherland."

An eyebrow quirked up. "Sutherland, is it? Are ye

fleeing Dunrobin, then?"

Fleeing Dunrobin? Her nape prickled again. Harder this time, as another couple of pieces of a puzzle began to fall into place. She was a history professor, but still. Her mind rejected the idea that was forming. She had better play it safe.

"I'm not sure what you mean."

"Cromartie and his men stormed Dunrobin nae long ago and Sutherland barely escaped. A lot of his kin fled too." He gave her an intense look. "Are ye one of them?"

More pieces of the puzzle rained down and began to fit. The Earl of Cromartie—aka George Mackenzie—commanded a brigade of Jacobites in the uprising in 1745.

It couldn't be. Could it?

She gave Robbie a cautious look. "Is there an arrest warrant out for Sutherlands?"

He frowned. "Nae that I ken." His expression smoothed out. "If that is what ye are afraid of, ye can relax. I have relatives on both sides of the conflict. If ye need a place to go to ground, my cousin Anne will take ye in."

"That's very kind of you, but…" Her voice trailed off.

"But? Ye have other plans?"

That was just it. She didn't. The streets were almost completely empty now and she had no idea where Thea and Charlotte might be. She wasn't even sure where she was. She had no money or place to shelter, either. "I'll admit, I am at a bit of a loss. Are you sure your cousin won't mind?"

He shook his head. "Anne will be glad to talk to a Sutherland. She always wants to ken what's happening in other places right now."

Vi wasn't sure how much information she could provide, but she could draw on her historical knowledge. "All right then, I'd be pleased to accept. Where does she live?"

"At Moy Hall. 'Tis nae far from here."

Moy Hall? It couldn't be! It just couldn't… Vi kept her facial expression neutral. "What is her last name?"

"Mackintosh, but she's from Clan Farquharson, as I am," Robbie gave her a wary look. "Do ye have a problem with that?"

"No." Vi suddenly gave him a smile. He had no idea of how heartfelt it was. Whatever had just taken place, it appeared she was in the eighteenth century and was about to meet Anne Farquharson-Mackintosh, the only female colonel in the entire Jacobite Army.

****

Robbie watched her covertly in the carriage taking them to Moy Hall. Most of his kin had piled into wagons to go home, so the only other occupants were a trio of older aunts, all of whom had imbibed a few drams of whisky and were in various stages of dozing off. One of them had given him a knowing look, while the other two had smiled and winked when he helped Vihansa into the carriage, and none of them had asked any questions. They probably assumed the lass with the flaming red hair was going to share his bed for the night.

His member stirred at the thought and he was glad it was too dark in the carriage for her to see the rise under his kilt. He promptly put his sporran over it anyhow.

"'Tis about ten miles to Moy Hall," he said. "If ye're tired, ye can rest your head on my shoulder."

There was no movement on her part and he could

11

have sworn he felt a draft of cold air suddenly waft toward him before she spoke. "I am fine, thank you."

Not the usual reaction he got from lasses. He wasn't sure if he wanted to frown or grin. Already he had gotten the impression that she had an independent spirit. He liked strong-willed women. They were always more exciting under the covers.

He frowned. This was not a lass he should be thinking about in that manner. She had fled Dunrobin with apparently only the clothing she wore. Who knew what ordeals she'd already overcome just to get to Inverness. What she needed was shelter and safety. His cousin would provide that, at least for now. Anne would also ferret out which side of the Cause Vihansa supported and act accordingly. Not that they weren't already a house divided, but he'd leave that mess to his cousin.

Meanwhile, he would get to know this goddess. How many women were interested in swords? She hadn't acted as if she were afraid of the weapon in spite of its lethality. The way she had touched the hilt—almost reverently—was unusual too. He had the distinct feeling that she was hiding something that didn't have to do with the war. At least, not the one being fought on Scottish soil. The War of Austrian Succession was taking place on the Continent and she'd said her mother had studied there. Her accent was strange, too. Was she somehow involved in foreign matters? She was obviously intelligent, and she'd already given her opinion on women leaders. His frown turned into a grin. He would find out what his goddess's secrets really were.

****

"Ye must be my new guest."

Vi turned from the window in the parlor, where she'd been enjoying the morning's pastoral view, to see Lady Anne Mackintosh standing in the doorway. At least, she assumed it was she. The portraits she'd seen online didn't do justice to her. Her hair was a soft auburn and cascaded in gloriously thick waves around her shoulders. She was slightly built, of medium height, and youthful-looking. Well, she *was* young…only twenty-three, if Vi recalled correctly. She hardly looked the part of a colonel in an army, which just proved that women shouldn't be stereotyped. It also explained—maybe—why Robbie hadn't asked more questions about her interest in weaponry.

"Lady Mackintosh?" Vi smiled and moved toward her. "I want to thank you for taking me in last night."

"'Tis what Highlanders do." Anne gestured toward the sofa while she took a seat in a nearby chair. "Robbie told me ye were fleeing from Dunrobin?"

Lady Mackintosh might not look like an army colonel, but she certainly sounded like one with the directness of that question. She hadn't wasted any time coming to the point. Vi liked that.

But how to answer the question? She hadn't had much time to absorb that she had apparently transported herself to the eighteenth century and she had no explanation of how or why. Not that she could share that information. It might be better—for now, at least—to go along with the story.

"I didn't want to be part of the spoils for Cromartie's men." She lifted one shoulder in a slight shrug. "I thought it better that I run than be raped."

"Understandable." Anne gave a curt nod. "Doona fash about it while ye are here, though. None of my men will bother ye."

And Anne's charm-the-ladies cousin? Would he ignore her? The thought leapt unbidden into Vi's mind. After her rather caustic reply to his invitation to use his shoulder for a pillow, he'd been quiet for the rest of the trip. She hadn't seen him this morning, only a maid had come by until Lady Mackintosh came into the room. *Not* that she wanted to encourage a flirtation. She knew his type too well.

"That's good to know."

"I apologize for nae being here to greet ye last night, but I was returning from Stirling." Anne watched her steadily. "I delivered several hundred troops to our Bonnie Prince Charlie."

Vi did a quick memory search. The Battle of Falkirk would take place in a fortnight or so and those must be the men she'd gathered to fight for the Cause but had to turn over since a woman couldn't lead troops. Vi wasn't sure how common the knowledge was that the prince was staying at Bannockburn, near Stirling, but she sensed Anne was testing her. She might as well be as direct as her hostess.

"Are you asking me which side I am on?"

For the first time, Anne smiled. "It might be good to ken." Her smile faded. "Just doona lie."

"I won't." She could at least be honest about this. "I want to see Scotland free."

Anne nodded and stood. "Then welcome to Moy Hall."

Vi stood too. "I will help you in any way I can."

She knew her history. She'd studied war strategy. Maybe she'd been sent back to the eighteenth century to help Anne turn the tide and Scotland would win after all.

Chapter Two

"Ye've certainly brought me a unique house guest." Anne poured a dram of whisky for Robbie and handed it to him before she sank down into the leather chair behind the big desk she used in the study. "It's been an interesting day."

"What happened?" he asked, settling in a chair closer to the fireplace but within easy speaking distance. "I wish I hadn't had to ride out, but since there was no sign of Redcoats around last night, I wanted to check our perimeters to make sure no ambush was in store."

Anne raised a brow. "Does that mean ye are going to side with me, after all?"

"I didna say that." Robbie sometimes felt he was being pulled in two different directions at once. His cousin supported the Jacobite cause while her husband, a captain in the Black Watch, supported the government. Even though Angus Mackintosh was away most of the time, Robbie was quite sure he was well aware of his wife's ambitions.

Not wanting to get into the middle of that unique situation, he tried not to take sides. Better to return to the subject.

"What happened today?" he asked again. "What did ye find out?"

"That's just it," Anne replied. "I didna find out much at all."

Robbie raised his own brows. "Ye are a master of ferreting."

"Thank ye." She frowned slightly. "I guess. With ye, I'm nae sure when something is a compliment or an insult."

"Ye wound me, cousin." Robbie put his hand over his heart. "Ye ken it was a compliment. Are ye wanting another one?"

"Nae." Anne waved a dismissive hand. "I probably wouldna believe ye anyway."

Robbie grinned, not bothering to dispute it. They'd grown up together and had spent most of their childhood bickering. Even though she was a full five years younger than he, she'd always held her own. Neither had she been one to be taken in by flattery even though he couldn't resist teasing her. He suspected that Vihansa wasn't susceptible either.

"So the lass gave nothing away?"

"Every time I asked something about her background, she countered with her own questions." She paused. "'Tis an interesting strategy. I'll have to think on using it myself."

"What kind of questions?"

Anne hesitated. "At first, it was general things like what kind of vegetables we'll be growing in the spring and the daily routine. Then she asked how I managed running Moy Hall with Angus away. If I had trouble getting any of our men to follow my orders. How I had managed to recruit several hundred men to support the prince—"

"What?" Robbie put down his glass and sat up straighter. "Do ye think she's gathering information for Sutherland?"

"I doona ken. My instinct is to say nae. She was quite adamant she felt Scotland should be a free country. We ken there has always been a question which side Sutherland's clan was truly on, even if he declared himself for the government. He wouldn't be the first to pay lip-service to King George."

"Aye. Our own neighbor, Simon Fraser, has done it often enough."

"True." Anne looked pensive. "Vihansa asked what I thought she could do to help."

Robbie frowned. "Did she ask to see any weapons?"

"Nae. Why would ye ask that?"

"She seemed to be fascinated with mine after we met. She wanted to touch it."

"While it was in its sheath?" Anne smirked at him. "I ken ye do encourage such things."

"Nae! I doona!" It sounded like a half-hearted protest even to his own ears since he remembered asking her what she'd be wanting. Then he remembered her response. "She actually wanted to see it. Hold it."

"Did ye let her?"

He scowled at Anne. "Sometimes I think ye think I'm a complete eejit."

She shrugged nonchalantly. "Sometimes ye are."

"Nae when it comes to weapons. I held it up. She stroked the hilt, almost like she were petting a pup or kit."

"Verra strange." Anne tapped her fingers on the desk. "'Tis nae like it was anything out of the ordinary, other than well-forged."

"Well... Och, I almost forgot." Robbie shook his head. "The lass did say she'd been taught to recognize good workmanship."

"Taught?" Anne gave him a sharp look. "Was Sutherland teaching women swordsmanship, then?"

"I doona ken. 'Twould be unlikely that she'd have run from Cromartie's troops, though, if she kenned how to fight."

"Nae necessarily," Anne replied. "Even if she can handle a sword, one against scores—even hundreds—is nae good odds."

Robbie nodded. "Especially for a woman." That earned him a glare from his cousin. "Doona get your feathers ruffled. Ye ken I'm right."

"Ye always think ye are right." Anne huffed a breath. "Although, I suppose, this *once*, I might agree with ye. Vihansa did say she'd rather run than be part of the victor's spoils."

"A wise decision." For some odd reason, the thought of Vihansa being another man's spoils made him want to punch something. Hard. He looked at the table beside him but managed to resist the urge.

Anne followed his look and smile mischievously. "The idea unsettles ye?"

He drew his brows together. "Of course, Why wouldna it? Women doona deserve to be raped."

"I canna argue that point, but I think maybe…" Her smile widened. "Ye have a wee bit more of a special interest?"

His frown deepened. His cousin was ferreting now. He was not about to let her know his thoughts. Especially since he wasn't sure himself what his thoughts regarding Vihansa were. She was an enigma.

****

Vihansa was admiring the assortment of weapons hung on the walls of the Great Hall the next morning when she heard footsteps behind her. Turning, she saw Robbie coming toward her. Since he'd been gone all day yesterday, she hadn't seen him since he'd brought her here from the Hogmanay festival.

He looked bigger in the light of day. Taller. Broader of shoulder. More muscular. His hair, curling slightly against the collar of the open shirt he wore, shone nearly blue-black as sunshine streaming in from the window struck him. The sunbeam also made his eyes a spectacular shade of blue, almost as though they were flashing blue flames. He'd be the perfect cover for one of Charlotte's romance novels. Looks could be deceiving, though. Hadn't she already found that out? Still. She needed to be polite since she was a guest here.

"Good morning."

He gave her that charming smile she remembered. "'Tis indeed, now that I ken ye are nae a figment of my imagination."

Was that flirtation she heard? Better to ignore it. She rather wished she were a figment, since then maybe she'd be awake in the twenty-first century. But that was neither here nor there for now. She was a firm believer in concentrating on the present.

"I believe I am in solid form."

He grinned, his eyes sweeping over her from head to toe and then, more slowly, back to her face. "I would agree on that, lass."

She felt her face warm. She hadn't meant that as an invitation, although it seemed she was prone to making unintended innuendos whenever she talked to him. She was usually quite precise in her speech, so what was it about him? Maybe her brain was still befuddled from apparently travelling through Time. That must be it. She turned back toward the wall and pointed.

"That is an interesting axe. Is it a Lochabre?"

"Aye."

"It looks quite old."

"'Tis from the first uprising, in 1689." He tilted his head. "If ye recognize it, ye must be truly named as goddess of warriors."

She didn't think he was flirting this time since he looked rather serious. "It's just a name. My mother's family came from...Prussia." She'd almost said Germany, which wasn't a country yet.

"Prussia," he said thoughtfully. "How long ago was that?"

Why would he ask such a question? Why would it be important? She zipped through her mental file. Ah. Currently, the War for Austrian Succession was taking place. The male line of the Habsburg dynasty had died out with Emperor Charles VI and his daughter, Maria-Theresa, reigned *suo jure*—in her own right—which was something the power-mad males of other countries were challenging. Not that it was surprising. Chauvinism was alive and kicking in the twenty-first century too. Back to the present—or past, depending on viewpoint—in 1745, Britain had allied itself with Austria and against Prussia, whose Frederick II was the greatest challenger to Maria Theresa. Which, to put a finish to her own thoughts, would put her on the wrong side of the conflict. However, Robbie was waiting for an answer.

"It was my grandparents who came. I'm not sure of the year." Better to change the subject before he started asking more questions. "Did one of your ancestors use this axe in the 1689 uprising?"

He nodded. "My great-uncle. He was determined to

keep James on the throne in spite of the king being a staunch Catholic amidst Protestants."

"Who probably weren't overly concerned since his daughter Mary married a Protestant and would reign when he died."

"Aye. Then James Francis Edward was born, and that changed the heir apparent."

Vi frowned. "Primogeniture never did make sense."

Robbie shrugged. "'Tis the way it's always been."

She wanted to tell him that Britain finally did ban the practice in 2011, but he would no doubt think her mad. Still. It rankled. "A first-born female should not be passed over for a younger brother."

"'Tis the way—"

"Which doesn't mean it can't change! Your cousin is a good example. Anne raised—by herself—several hundred men to fight for the prince, yet she had to let Alex MacGillivray of Clan Chattan lead them because *men* think women don't have the ability." She frowned. "You agree, don't you?"

He gave her a slow smile. "I think I would be a real eejit to answer that."

She glared at him. "You think women are inferior!"

His smile widened. "What I think, lass, is that ye are prickly as a thistle."

"I am...*not*."

"Hmmm."

His noncommittal tone irked her almost as much as if he had agreed with her statement, but before she could retort, he spoke.

"Ye ken that Mary did succeed James to the throne, aye?" He grinned again. "From all accounts, she was a woman."

Did he think she was stupid? She taught European history! Vi gave herself a mental shake. Of course, he couldn't know that. So she smiled sweetly. "I am aware. I also know that if William had not co-ruled with her, Glen Coe may not have happened."

The grin faded and Robbie gave her an appraising look. "King William needed the allegiance of the MacDonalds, since he was a foreigner."

"My point exactly." She felt a little triumphant. "If Mary had ruled in her own right, she wouldn't have had to have allegiance pledged! There would have been no slaughter."

"And if James had nae been deposed, his son would have taken the throne and we'd nae be here in the middle of another war."

Vi opened her mouth to reply, then snapped it shut. He was right, damn it.

He studied her again, then extended his hand. "Truce, lass?"

She looked at the large, strong, tanned hand with its white scar slashes. The result of other fights, no doubt. "Truce." As she took his hand, the same odd tingle—not *the* tingle, but the other one she'd felt—shot through her.

****

Her hand felt so small and smooth in his even through her grip was amazingly strong for a lass. For a moment, as they stood with their hands clasped tightly together, eyes locked, he wondered if she wanted to engage in a tug of war. He'd win, of course. All he had to do was one yank and she'd be in his arms, close enough to kiss…and probably have his teeth loosened by a slap across his face.

Robbie released her hand and watched as a range of

emotions crossed her face. Some of them seemed to mirror his own feelings, because he really did not know what to think about her. He was not used to women being cross with him or even contradicting him, for that matter. *Most* lasses liked his company, even vying for being the first to dance with him or sit beside him at a gathering. That was just fact. But Vihansa seemed to take pleasure in arguing with him. He wasn't sure whether to be annoyed or challenged by her apparent disinterest in him. He didn't like feeling confused.

He realized he was standing there like a moonstruck calf. She had asked about the Lochabre axe before their conversation had been diverted. He reached for it now, taking it carefully off the wall.

"Highlanders used this kind in their charge."

"I know. The hook on the end of the blade is particularly effective in pulling a cavalry man from his horse."

Robbie gave her a quizzical look. "How do ye ken about that?"

She turned a bit pink. "Ah...I heard the men at Sutherland's talking about the strategy. That they'd have to be careful to keep close ranks."

He frowned. "Sutherland was expecting to send his cavalry out at Dunrobin?"

"Ah... Well, he wasn't sure what the Jacobites had in mind." She looked a little distraught. "Better to be prepared, I guess."

There was something not quite right with her answer, but he couldn't pin it down. From what he'd heard, the attack at Dunrobin had been totally unexpected. The government soldiers would not have had time to send their cavalry out. Sutherland himself escaped through a postern gate. Robbie supposed the men might have been discussing future tactics at some point, but again, they'd felt Dunrobin a safe haven. The lass did seem to be particularly knowledgeable, though. Something he would ponder on later.

He lifted the long-handled axe a bit higher. "My da told me my great-uncle was verra proud of this axe."

"I would think he would be." Vi reached out to run her fingers along the five-foot polished wood staff to which the axe head was attached and tilted her head to view the sharp, curved edge of the blade. "It looks remarkably well preserved."

"Aye. When Anne married the Mackintosh, she brought this with her." He gestured toward several other weapons on the wall. "Those belong to the Farquharsons as well."

"Smart of your cousin to give her husband a subtle hint that her own clan is strong." Vi smiled. "She probably knows how to use them, too."

"I doona ken." Vihansa was eyeing the poleaxe speculatively and Robbie replaced it on the wall before she decided she wanted to try it out. It was bad enough when she'd wanted to handle his sword. He doubted she'd be able to wield the axe because of its weight and length, but she could probably do just as much damage by struggling to hold it and letting it slip. Then an image of Vihansa—dressed in a tunic and leather lacings as the goddess she was named after—brandishing both weapons while charging the enemy inserted itself into his thoughts. Robbie gave himself an inward shake and almost laughed.

"What are you snickering about?" She sounded defensive.

So she was back to being annoyed with him. He wasn't about to tell her of the image that had flashed through his mind. He straightened his mouth. "Nothing important."

She gave him a suspicious look, but to his eternal gratitude, she remained silent as they left. He certainly couldn't tell her how arousing the image of her as a warrior goddess had been.

****

Robbie Farquharson had to be one of the most exasperating men she'd ever known. In *either* century. Not that she'd been in *this* century that long. Still. One moment they could be having an interesting, intelligent conversation about a traditional weapon historically used by Scots, and the next, she got the distinct impression he was trying not to laugh at her. He probably thought she had no idea of how to handle a halberd-type axe or use a sword or even swing a claymore.

She hated that she hemmed and hawed around him, too, and couldn't seem to get a coherent sentence straight, like when he'd questioned her about Sutherland's cavalry. Although, in her own defense, she had been forced to make that up as she went along, and she wasn't good at making up stories. Leave that to Charlotte. But she'd felt discombobulated after the dance when he'd intimated that she'd been staring at a manly part of his anatomy. She'd only made it worse by her response when she'd just wanted to find out if his sword was the portal back to the twenty-first century. A perfectly natural request, given her circumstances.

Yes, she couldn't deny there was something about Robbie…she'd never felt a tingle when she'd touched a man's hand before, not even with Matt. With Robbie, she felt like a piece of kindling that only needed a spark to ignite. Maybe that was why her temper seemed so short with him. He both infuriated her and intrigued her. It was quite unsettling.

Chapter Three

"In the week that ye've been here, I am beginning to think ye will live up to your name." Anne grounded her sword and laughed.

Vihansa grounded hers as well. For the past few days, they'd been practicing fencing in the courtyard. The first time, men had gathered around, and although they'd shown great respect for Anne, they'd smirked at her. No doubt they thought she couldn't hold her own. That had quickly changed. It was too bad Robbie had gone to Lochaber for a meeting of the Clan Chattan confederation.

She grinned. "I take it you are referencing the warrior and not the goddess part?"

"Depends." Anne started back to the house. "We could use divine intervention right now."

"I wish I could help with that." Vi picked up her hat from the ground, plopped it on her head, and fell into step beside Anne. "I'm afraid my only claim to the divine is my mother's fancy."

"Robbie mentioned that you said your mother had studied in Prussia?"

"Yes" She was going to have be careful that she didn't put herself on the wrong side of the Succession War. "Both Prussia and Austria, actually."

"I guess that was before they were fighting each other?"

"They weren't fighting each other when she was there." That much was true since it had happened at the millennium. "Things were peaceful."

Anne gave her a sideways look. "Were ye with your mother?"

Vi hesitated. She had recently spent time—in the twenty-first century—visiting both Germany and Austria, although that wasn't relevant. However, if she admitted to visiting *Prussia* and Austria—in this century—perhaps she could offer some advice as to military strategy that the Jacobites could use. They were going to need it before Culloden happened and she had the historical knowledge to provide that information.

"Actually, I was with her there. When my father passed away, my mother wanted to go back and spend some time." That was true as well, except for leaving out the time period.

"I'm sorry to hear that. Did your mother return with ye?"

Vi shook her head. "My mother took ill several years ago and didn't recover." Also true, thanks to the pandemic.

"How sad. 'Tis nae easy to be an orphan at any age." Anne gave her a sympathetic look. "So William Sutherland took ye in?"

William—ah, yes. The Earl of Sutherland. For a moment, thinking about her parents, Vi had forgotten it was the 1700s. She nodded, since she really didn't have another choice. "I'm really distant kin." That much was true, at least.

"In Scotland, kin is kin. 'Tis nae a matter of how distant."

Vi smiled. "I have always liked the idea of Highland

hospitality, even if the guest in question is not a friend."

Anne shrugged. "The Highlands are beautiful, but they are harsh. To nae offer shelter and food would be the most dishonorable thing a clan could do."

Vi remembered her conversation with Robbie about King William and the massacre of the MacDonalds. "And if it backfires like at Glen Coe?"

"Then the shame is on them." Anne grimaced. "Even if the Campbells were nae King George's men, they would nae be welcome in these parts because of that betrayal."

"At least King George is somewhat occupied with Austria's War of Succession."

Anne nodded. "Since France invaded Flanders several years ago, George is more concerned that it will overrun the Austrian Netherlands and eventually threaten the Hanoverian dynasty."

"So it's for his own ends that Britain is defending Austria."

"Always." Anne grimaced. "That's why Charles Stuart is a threat to him too. The English king doesn't want to relinquish any so-called sovereign territory."

"Well, his preoccupation with the continental wars is giving the prince time to gather soldiers and accumulate some victories."

"Aye. Prestopans was a great victory." Anne frowned. "I heard the prince is nae doing as well with getting Glasgow to submit, even though he's hosting balls and such."

"It is not really surprising, is it?" Vi tried to tread carefully, not wanting to sound overly knowledgeable. "Since Glasgow is closer to the English border, a lot of its politicians lean toward King George."

Anne sighed. "We can only hope they'll see the light when the French troops arrive and bolster the prince's reserves."

Some of those troops weren't going to make it, including one ship that would sink, but Vi didn't want to be the harbinger of bad news. There was nothing she could do to prevent that, and history would play itself out. Still, some of King Louis' soldiers would make it over, at least during this first round. "I hope seeing the French soldiers arrive will bolster morale."

"I do too." Anne paused. "My fear, though, is that King George may recall his brother from Flanders to stop them from getting here."

That would happen as well. The Duke of Cumberland would become known at "The Butcher" for his *give-no-quarter* policies. But that was information Vi wasn't about to impart either. And…possibly, just possibly, some of that killing could be prevented if she were successful in changing the strategy for the Battle of Culloden.

"Let's hope that doesn't happen."

"I wish Robbie would get back from the conference," Anne said. "We'll ken more about what is being planned then."

Vi was about to respond when she heard a thundering of hooves and turned to see a dusty rider come through the gate. As if Anne had conjured him, it was Robbie.

The real strategy of the next few months was about to begin, and Vi needed to be able to take part. That might be easier said than done, given that their communication had been somewhat cantankerous before he left. That wasn't going to stop her, though. Vi sheathed the sword she'd been carrying, lifted her chin and walked with Anne to meet him.

****

As he rode into the courtyard, Robbie spotted Anne, dressed in her split-skirt riding habit, but he didn't recognize the person beside her until the wind blew the hat off and Vihansa's bright hair flared like loose flames around her face. For a moment, when he saw her sheath her sword with her hair swirling, an image of a warrior queen flitted through his mind. Then he frowned. What was she doing yielding a sword? And wearing men's clothing?

"Welcome back," Anne said as he dismounted and handed the reins to a stable lad. "Have ye news?"

He nodded absently as he looked Vihansa over, noting that the trews she wore were a bit too small and outlined shapely legs and an even shapelier backside. His frown deepened. She'd been parading around the men in the courtyard like that?

"Why are ye wearing trews?"

One eyebrow lifted slightly as did her chin. "Anne and I have been fencing."

"Ye are dressed like a man."

The high brow went higher. "You expect me to wear a gown when I'm practicing with a sword?"

"I doona expect ye to practice with a sword at all." He looked over to his cousin. "What has been going on while I've been gone?"

"Nae much and ye can stop glowering. Ye'll scare the wee ones."

"Wee ones?" He looked over her shoulder to see several of the women who worked at Moy Hall shepherding small children back into the house. "What

31

are they doing out here?"

Vihansa answered before Anne could. "Their mothers brought them out to watch us at swordplay."

"To watch—" He stopped himself and took a breath. "Why would ye be wantin' to do that?"

"To set an example, of course," Vi answered. "Children should know that women can protect themselves."

"And ye may need protection, with the way the men were ogling ye." He turned to Anne. "What has happened to your common sense, cousin?"

"It is perfectly intact." Anne was unfazed by his outburst. "The men have seen me practicing with a sword before."

"But ye are nae dressed like…like a…" He caught himself before he blurted out the word *vixen,* "like a *man*." By all that was holy, if Vihansa could addle his brains in those tight trews, what was she doing to the other men?

"In case you haven't noticed, your cousin and I are hardly the same size," Vihansa said. "so I borrowed these pants from one of the stable boys."

He nearly groaned aloud. No doubt the lad was enjoying bragging rights in the stables even as they stood here speaking. Had it been Jamie, the blacksmith's nephew who was already attracting the lasses? He'd come to take his horse earlier and been smiling quite readily… He forced the thought from his mind. He could find the willing culprit later. "'Tis nae proper."

Vihansa started to sputter, but Anne intervened. "In case ye have nae noticed, cousin, verra few things around Moy Hall are *proper*. My husband is off fighting for the English while I fight for Scotland. I am nae a doting wife either, content to sit with mending and planning menus."

"'Tis different."

"Nae. Many of our men have already joined the prince's cause. The men who remain are ready to leave at a moment's notice, if necessary. I agree completely that women need to be able to protect themselves." She smiled warmly at Vihansa, then turned back to him. "Vihansa has been a blessing. I am so glad she's here."

Robbie bit back another groan. He was beginning to wonder if the Fates were playing with him.

****

And to think, she'd *almost* been glad to see Robbie. Almost. Then he had to go and make a chauvinistic remark about her wearing pants. If only he knew what women wore—or how little they wore—in the twenty-first century! She'd love to see the expression on his face if she were to take him back…

Wait. Take him back? To the present day? She wasn't sure where that thought had come from, but it was provocative. She could just see him marching down the street in the ritzy Dallas suburb of Highland Park— which wasn't on a hill, had nothing to do with real Highlanders but a lot to do with old money—dressed in his kilt and brazenly telling women wearing a thousand-dollar pair of Jimmy Choo stilettos that their ankles were showing. She gave a self-satisfied nod at the mental image and smiled.

"I am glad ye agree with me then," Robbie said.

Vi broke out of her reverie to stare at Robbie. What was she agreeing to? Oh. He'd just remarked that it wasn't proper of her to have borrowed the pants. Her smile faded. "I certainly do not agree with you." On anything, she wanted to add, since she was remembering he'd also said she shouldn't be practicing with a sword, either.

A corner of his mouth quirked up. "'Tis a common assumption, lass, that when someone nods and smiles, that person is in agreement with what was said."

She knew that. Did he think her addled? Of course, if she told him what she'd really been thinking about, he *would* think her addled, for sure. She tried to shake off her jumble of thoughts. What was it about him that always made her flustered? It wasn't like her at all. She lifted her chin.

"I was thinking about what Anne said. Not all women are content to be relegated to kitchens and bedrooms."

The quirk widened into a grin. "I doona recall my cousin mentioning bedrooms."

Vi felt her face warm. Damn it. He was doing it again. Making her feel disconcerted. She'd been referring to the old adage of "barefoot and pregnant," but she managed to stop herself from saying that. She'd only sound more befuddled. Besides, she doubted the adage was even known in the eighteenth century. The two conditions were more like factual.

"What I meant was—"

"Ye doona have to explain, lass. I ken what matters take place in kitchens and…" He paused, his grin widening once more. "…and bedrooms," he finished. He glanced around and lowered his voice conspiratorially, even though there was no one there but the three of them. "Mayhap 'tis a discussion best held elsewhere?"

"Elsewhere?" Did he mean *in* the bedroom? An odd warmth washed over her. She hadn't thought about *bedrooms* since she'd tossed Matt out of hers. Then, seeing the twinkle in Robbie's eyes, she realized he was teasing her. Or mocking, more likely. She frowned. "I think the discussion is quite finished."

"And I agree." Anne had been standing quietly by during their interchange. "I'd rather know what took place at the conference. So, instead of having our people speculate what we're doing out here, I suggest we go in."

****

His assumption about Vihansa had been right, Robbie thought as he followed her and his cousin into the house. The lass *was* prickly as a thistle. What had she been thinking, strutting around the courtyard in form-fitting trews for all the men—not to mention green stable lads—to observe her womanly assets? Even now, as they were leaving the courtyard, he could see the lads piled up by the stables' doors, and it seemed that the adult men were also managing to keep themselves busy in full sight of Vihansa. Had she no idea of the furor she was causing? Instinctively, he stepped closer, shielding her delectable backside from being seen, and promptly bumped into her when she stopped suddenly.

"What do you think you are doing?" she asked.

"I'm following ye into the house."

"You are breathing down my neck."

A slight breeze drifted across the courtyard just then and he picked up a slight citrusy scent, similar to their orangery, wafting upward from the open collar of her shirt. It was unlike the florals most lasses wore, but maybe he shouldn't be surprised since the tartness fitted her more than a fragile flower did. He also caught the faint musky smell of *woman* and, unexpectedly, his loins stirred. He shifted his position so she wouldn't notice. The scent probably came from her exertion at swordplay, but it made him think of a hearty and lengthy romp in bed, with tangled sheets damp because of their endeavors. What was she doing to him? He rarely let his thoughts run wild like that. At least not unless the lass he was with encouraged that line of thinking. Which Vihansa obviously did *not*. She'd already turned away from him, and he stared at her retreating back. Then he frowned. The shirt she was wearing was a man's. She'd obviously borrowed that too.

Anne stopped near the door and turned toward him. "Are you coming?"

"Aye." Who had Vihansa borrowed that shirt from? Jamie? He started walking. He would find out.

Meanwhile, while he might be fighting his own private little battle with Vihansa, Scotland was at war, and he did have important information to relay.

Chapter Four

The room Anne led them to was at the back of the Great Hall, accessible through a door behind the dais that could be secured with a heavy wood-and-iron bolt. The room had a secondary door, hidden from view by a large tapestry depicting the scenes of a hunt. When Vi had first seen it, she'd smiled at the irony of the hunt scene since the second door was really an escape, should Moy Hall be breeched and the Mackintoshes find themselves being "hunted." It opened into a hidden passageway that led down to the cellars and then out through a postern gate. The whole thing was quite medieval and probably based on the design of the original Moy Castle on an island in Loch Moy. Of course, the modern-day structure, built in the 1950s, looked nothing like this one—and Vi doubted it had any hidden passageways, either.

Surprisingly, though, the room was comfortable. Even without windows—Anne called it her secured room—it didn't feel claustrophobic, probably because numerous wall sconces gave the room a soft glow. An oblong table at one end seated twelve—the number of clans in the Chattan Confederation, Vi had been told—and there were also cabinets, bookcases, and an escritoire on that end. The other half of the room was arranged like a parlor, with comfortable arm chairs in a semicircle facing a small hearth.

"So what is the word from the confederation

conference?" Anne asked after they were all seated.

"It started with the usual clan business," Robbie replied, "and then there were the pledges of allegiance to the Cause."

"Did everyone agree?" Anne asked.

"Nae at first. There were some, like myself, who still question sacrificing our lads for something we might not be able to win."

Vi snapped her head up, hoping her ears weren't pricking like a pointer dog. She knew that not all Highlanders favored the Stuart prince—her own Sutherland ancestors were an example—but this was the first she'd heard that Robbie might not be a fervent believer. And, of course, if she couldn't wield some influence, he would be right.

"You don't think Scotland can win this war?"

"'Tis nae whether *Scotland* can win." He paused as if trying to gather his thoughts and finally spoke. "'Tis whether the prince will heed the wisdom of his elders."

"I have heard," Vi said carefully, not wanting to sound traitorous, "that Prince Charlie tends to be a bit hot-headed."

Robbie gave her a long look. "Arrogant is a word I heard used by some."

"He is young," Anne interjected. "I'm sure General Murray will make him see sense."

Robbie switched his gaze to her. "That seems to be the problem. The prince and Murray are already at odds."

When Vi thought about it, perhaps it wasn't so unusual that Prince Charlie would be skeptical of George Murray, who was the son of the Duke of Atholl. The man had originally pledged allegiance to King George and had supported the 1707 Union before deciding to join the

Jacobites. But having been on both sides lent a certain amount of expertise and wisdom. She'd have to ponder on that later, since she didn't want to miss the conversation.

Anne frowned. "How? What happened to set them at odds?"

"I am nae sure."

Anne's frown deepened. "The siege for Stirling is still planned, is it nae? The prince should be pleased, I would think."

He paused. "Ye have had nae word on Falkirk, then?"

"None." Anne sat up ramrod in her chair. "What took place?"

Vi could have told them from what she'd read in history books, but she was too curious to listen to discussion of the actual event as it happened in real time. She looked at Robbie in anticipation, her annoyance with him forgotten, at least momentarily.

"I'll start at the beginning, then."

"Always wise," Vi murmured, mostly to herself, but it drew a sharp look from Robbie anyway.

"Ye ken morale has been high since Christmas and the battle at Inverurie. Drummond's recruits have been near Stirling since then."

What Vi found fascinating was the casual mention of names, although they would have been well known in this time. John Drummond was the Duke of Perth, but he was also Franco-Scottish and had managed to get both money and weapons from King Louis, and he'd brought back a contingency of Irish and French soldiers. His official rank was Lieutenant General, second only to George Murray.

"Shortly after ye sent your troops to the prince, the main army under Murray left Glasgow for Stirling where they were to rendezvous with Drummond. The plan was to march on Falkirk and then turn north towards the castle. The rest of the army marched through Bannockburn where the prince is headquartered." Robbie shrugged nonchalantly. "It didna take long for the town of Stirling to surrender."

Vi couldn't resist egging him a bit. "I daresay the castle wasn't quite so easy?"

Robbie raised a brow and studied her before answering. "Ye are correct. The garrison there was under command of an Irish veteran named Blakeney. The siege began on the eighth, but he managed to hold fast."

"So the siege is underway then?" Anne asked.

"'Tis done."

Vi wondered if Robbie were deliberately playing out the story to keep Anne—and herself, she might as well admit it—intrigued.

"Done? Ye are beginning to vex me, Robbie. Tell me what happened."

Vi managed not to burst out laughing. She couldn't have said it better.

He gave both of them a rather annoyed look. "The English general—Hawley—decided to send seven thousand English troops to advance on Stirling since it was under siege. They arrived on the fifteenth and camped just outside of town. When he didn't attack the castle on the sixteenth, Murray decided to take the offensive."

"Go on," Anne said.

"Some of Drummond's men marched toward Stirling to distract Hawley's men while Murray took a position on the high ground to the south above the camp."

Vi suppressed a smile. It was typical medieval war strategy to obtain the high position since it was easier to attack going downhill and easier to defend against the enemy coming *uphill,* which was why medieval castles were also built with winding staircases wider on the right side ascending since it limited an enemy's ability to draw or wield his sword. But she was digressing into former research and Robbie was talking.

"Hawley's mistake was thinking the Jacobites wouldn't dare attack him at his camp a mile away." Robbie snorted. "Typical English."

"When did he realize his folly?" Anne asked.

"Nae till late in the afternoon. The weather suddenly changed and what started out as rain changed to heavy snow and a strong wind blowing into Hawley's troops." Robbie grinned. "Ye can count on Scottish weather for that."

"Will ye *please* go on, cousin."

"Give a man time to enjoy the tellin' of it, would ye?" Robbie grumbled. "The English started up the slope to the ridge with their cavalry leading…" He grinned again suddenly. "I guess they didna learn their lesson at Prestopans, aye?"

Vi had to admit that Robbie did have a knack for holding his audience in suspension. Although maybe Prestopans wasn't such a mystery in this time. Basically, the English sent their horses through a marshy area where they were bogged down and the English under John Cope weren't prepared for a Highland Charge. The battle only lasted thirty minutes. Vi grimaced, and Robbie gave her an inquisitive look.

"What is it, lass?"

She shook her head. "Nothing." She couldn't tell him that the Battle of Culloden wouldn't last much longer than that but with a completely different outcome if she couldn't intervene somehow. "Just thinking about the horses."

"Aye. They churned the ground into a muddy mess and the infantry had trouble plowing through it. The rain and snow also affected the black powder cartridges, causing the muskets to misfire."

"So it was an easy victory?" Anne asked.

Robbie shook his head. "Nae quite."

"Why?"

"Well, Murray was commanding the right flank just opposite where the dragoons had halted by the ridge. He marched with the MacDonalds to form a battle line, instructing that they hold their fire until he gave the order. Meanwhile, Drummond, who was supposed to be leading the left flank, was nowhere to be seen. Murray asked the prince to name an alternative commander, but the prince refused."

Vi sighed. This was just one example of how a twenty-something prince was not taking the advice of a hardened, experienced general. She knew Drummond did show up shortly after, but it would be a bitter point of contention with Murray.

"Then what happened?" Anne asked.

"The weather was closing in and getting worse," Robbie continued, "but the English commander Ligonier ordered his three regiments to attack the MacDonalds anyway. They didna fire until the redcoats were within pistol range and then it took only one volley to have them turn tail and scatter."

"That sounds like a victory to me," Anne said dryly.

"'Twas, but instead of going ahead and attacking Hawley's right, the MacDonalds charged down the hill and looted the English camp. With the blowing snow and dusk setting on, Murray couldna tell who was where."

"So he called it off?"

"He had nae choice, really. Meanwhile, the English held their positions on the right, pushing the Scots back. 'Tis sorry I am to say it, but the Jacobites fled all the way back to Stirling." He paused. "They didna ken the left had been routed, so they put about the news that the prince had lost the day."

Anne's mouth set in a hard line. "'Tis bad news, then."

"Nae all of it," Robbie replied. "Most of Hawley's men fled too. They were seen on the road to Edinburgh, and Captain Cunningham, who was in charge of the English artillery, abandoned the guns and used the transport horses to flee the scene as well. So," Robbie shrugged and gave them a half-smile. "We Scots won the day after all."

"With too much confusion," Anne said.

Vi couldn't have agreed with her more. Besides the young prince's stubbornness, poor command and lack of coordination almost cost the Jacobites the battle. Murray would blame Drummond for being late and Drummond would blame Murray for not ordering the MacDonalds to press on. The squabbling would be a problem that would continue to plague the movement and ultimately cause defeat at Culloden.

Unless she somehow could change the outcome of that.

Chapter Five

Robbie left the breakfast room the next morning feeling quite content. Not only was he well fed, he was feeling good about the outcome at Falkirk and looking forward to the ceilidh celebration Anne was planning. It would be good to laugh and dance and feel carefree for an evening. He was quite looking forward to dancing with Vihansa. He could picture her now in a silk gown with a skirt that swirled around both of them as he spun her about and then pulled her close...

His reverie was broken by the clash of swords in the courtyard. Rounding the corner, he saw Vihansa dressed not in a gown of any sort, but the tight-fitting trews again. She had her back to him and he could see her plump bottom all too well. And, instead of sparring with Anne, she was engaged in sword play with Jamie, the blacksmith's nephew. Robbie narrowed his eyes. *Had* Jamie been the one to lend her his trews?

He scowled and stomped toward them. Jamie must have seen his face because the lad's own went pale and he dropped his sword.

"Why did you do that?" Vi halted her lunge halfway, her sword still in the air.

"Ah...ah..."

"Because he should be working, that's why," Robbie all but thundered behind her.

Vihansa pivoted, the point of her sword leveled at

his stomach. It was a little too close for comfort, but Robbie refused to flinch. "Ye mind putting that down?"

For a moment, he wondered if she would. She looked like she might be contemplating running him through with it. Then, to his relief—not that he'd show it—she grounded the point.

"What do you think you are doing?"

"Keeping ye from getting hurt, obviously." He turned to Jamie. "Do ye nae have horses to tend to?"

"Aye, I do." He looked at the sword lying in the dust, started to reach for it, then glanced nervously at Robbie. "I should take the weapon back into the hall."

"Just leave it."

He nodded and moved away. Robbie was pretty sure the lad wanted to break into a run, but to Jamie's credit, he walked. Albeit it quickly.

He turned his attention back to Vihansa only to find her glaring at him as she spoke. "Why did you do that?"

"Because..." He was beginning to feel rather foolish—and a little guilty—for being so harsh. "The lad has a job to do."

"The horses have all been fed." Vihansa looked around the courtyard pointedly. "I don't see anyone waiting for one of them to be saddled."

"'Tis nae the point," Robbie said stubbornly. "It sets a bad example for the other stable lads."

Vihansa gave an exasperated sigh. "Have you thought that maybe—just maybe—those stable lads need to learn to handle a sword?" She waved a hand at the empty courtyard. "Most of Anne's soldiers are at Stirling." She sharpened her gaze on him. "You do remember telling us about the battle yesterday?"

He scowled again. "Of course I do." Did the lass

think him an eejit? Completely daft? "What does that have to do with anything?"

The look she gave him made him think maybe she *was* thinking he was completely daft. "The battle is nae being fought here."

Another sigh. This one sounded longsuffering, as if she were thinking of a way to explain something that should be obvious. Only it wasn't. "What?"

"Has it occurred to you…" She paused as though giving him time to let the words sink in. "…that the battle could turn and we would need to be able to defend ourselves?"

"We are too far north. Hawley's men are running back to Edinburgh."

Vihansa opened her mouth, then shut it, apparently holding back her retort. He gave her a benevolent smile in return. "Doona fash, lass. We have neighbors who would come to our aid until the prince's army arrives."

She didn't answer, but she didn't smile either. Instead, she pointed to the sword lying on the ground. "You might as well pick that up."

"Aye." He bent to get it and started to turn around. "I'll take it to the weaponry room."

"Wait." Before he could turn back she had come around to face him. "I wasn't through practicing. You can take Jamie's place."

He stared at her, wondering if maybe his mind was addled after all. "I'll nae fight a woman."

"I am not asking you to fight," she said in the patient tone one might use with a none-too-bright child. "I am asking you to practice with me."

"Nae."

"Why not?"

"Because you are a woman." He let his eyes scan her. "And ye really should nae be wearing trews."

"*What*?"

For a moment, he could have sworn that her hair crackled around her. It certainly seemed to flare a more brilliant red. Maybe he had pushed a bit too hard. He decided to use a dulcet, calming voice. "I am sure Anne can have one of her riding habits altered."

Vihansa obviously wasn't mollified, because her eyes started shooting sparks too. "I *like* wearing trews. They're comfortable."

She was going to argue with him? He narrowed his eyes. "Whose trews are they, anyway? Jamie's?"

For a moment, she just stared at him. Then she shook her head. "Male chauvinist," she muttered, and then she walked away, not heeding his call to wait.

He grimaced, realizing he was standing alone in the courtyard and talking to himself since Vihansa had disappeared.

What was it about her that made him act like a green lad anyway?

****

Anne looked up from the notes she was writing when Vihansa walked into the room she used as a study, at the back of the house.

"Is something amiss?"

Yes. She'd just had the most infuriating conversation with the insufferable Robbie Farquharson. Who did he think he was, ending her fencing practice and then telling her not to wear trews? *And*, to add insult, he refused to take a position against her *because* she was a woman. If only she could tell him women *now* served in combat units.

But this wasn't "now," at least not the twenty-first century version of it. She sank into the chair in front of Anne's desk.

"No. Nothing's amiss."

"Your face is quite red. Did Jamie wear ye out in practice?"

Ha! Jamie didn't get to practice with her. Her face probably looked like a sunset, though, the bane of fair-skinned redheads when they got angry. She took a deep breath and forced herself to calm down. Somewhat, anyhow.

"Your cousin didn't think Jamie should be practicing with me."

"Ah."

"And he doesn't think I should wear trews either."

"Ah," Anne laid her pen down and leaned back in her chair. "I guess ye didna agree with him?"

"Of course not! Trews are practical and comfortable. Why shouldn't I wear them?" Vi tried not to sound petulant. "But I am more upset about him not allowing me to practice with Jamie. The boy has a natural feel for the weapon."

Anne raised a brow. "Jamie is nigh unto twenty."

Vi paused. He certainly didn't look that age. She'd thought him to be no more than fifteen or so. Still. "If he's that old, I'm surprised he is not off with the other soldiers you sent to the prince."

"Oh, he wanted to go." Anne looked out the window near her desk with a pensive expression and then back at Vihansa. "His brother was killed at Prestopans and his mother begged Robbie not to let him go."

"So…Robbie forbade him to go?"

Anne shook her head. "Although Jamie is young,

he's a grown man. Robbie didn't forbid him. He just asked him who would take care of his mother and his sister if he were killed too. There are no other male siblings and the father died several years ago. His uncle, Don Fraser—our blacksmith—didn't want him leaving either, since he's been training him there."

"Oh." Still…had it been Robbie who guilted the boy into staying? Or had he just been pointing out the obvious with common sense? Vi wasn't sure. The high-handed Robbie she'd just had an argument with didn't mesh well with any image of a more understanding man. She frowned. "He gave Jamie quite a tongue-lashing just now."

"Robbie tends to bluster a bit." Anne eyed her. "Am I correct in guessing the two of ye had a wee bit of a discussion as well?"

"I'm not sure you'd call it a discussion." When Anne didn't answer, she went on.

"I don't like being told what to do…or, in this case, what *not* to do."

"Would ye like for me to speak to him about it?"

"*No!* Thank you for the thought, but *no*." God forbid that his cousin would defend her as though she were a helpless child. "It's just that your cousin seems to enjoy irritating me."

"I'll nae argue that point, since he can annoy me too." Anne tilted her head to study her. "I think ye are an enigma to him, though."

"Me? Why?"

"The lasses around here are quite taken with Robbie, and he kens it." Anne smiled. "And he doesna ken quite what to do with one who isna enamored over him."

Vi frowned. "I wouldn't be enamored over any

man."

Anne's smile widened suddenly. "And 'tis another reason I am glad ye are here."

Vi smiled too, her mood lightening. "What are you working on?"

"Preparations for the ceilidh. I always forget how much work is involved." Anne picked up a sheaf of papers and shuffled them. "Make sure we have enough beeswax candles, clean the glass sconces, bring in fresh rushes, make sure the stables are clean with enough hay for extra horses, meet with Cook, prepare a menu and inventory what food needs to be ordered, arrange for a hunt, get the meat cooked, arrange for musicians, and," she held up a final paper, "make sure I don't leave anyone off the guest list."

"Is there anything I can help with?"

"Hmmm." Anne flipped through the papers again. "I may send ye in to Inverness with Cook for the food. Two of ye can pick up the things faster than one."

"I'll be glad to go. I can help with cooking, as well."

Anne shook her head. "Ye'd be wise to stay well away from the kitchen once Cook gets started. She turns into a field general, and the staff is trained on what to do, especially the last-minute finishing touches. Besides, ye'll be wanting to get yourself dressed and ready for the party."

"Um…I hadn't planned on attending."

"What?" Anne laid down the papers. "Why ever nae? We eat until we're stuffed, we dance until we drop… 'Twill be a night to remember, I vow."

Vi remembered the two women who had draped themselves over Robbie at the Hogmanay dance. Given what Anne had just said, she could envision a whole row—maybe several rows—of local girls lined up, waiting to dance with the miscreant. Not that she cared, but it would be boring to watch. But Anne was waiting for an answer. At least she could use her name as an excuse.

"You're celebrating Prince Charlie's victory at Falkirk." Vi shrugged. "It would be better for me not to put in an appearance because I don't think Sutherlands are any more welcome in these parts than Campbells."

Anne frowned. "Has anyone here made ye feel unwelcome?"

Vi shook her head. "Not here, but you're inviting neighbors from surrounding clans who may resent me, even though I support your cause."

"Doona fash about that." Anne smiled. "Two years ago, when Angus was approached by Earl Loudoun to head up one of the Black Watch companies, I secured ninety-seven of the hundred men needed for my husband to be a captain. Then, last year when Prince Charlie arrived in Scotland, I switched my alliance and raised over three hundred and fifty men for the cause."

Vi had always thought that was one of the most interesting episodes of the entire Scottish fight for independence. "I'd love to hear that story sometime."

Anne nodded. "Sometime. But what's important for ye to ken right now is that a number of clans—like the Murrays—are split in their loyalties. Some even prefer to be neutral."

Vi wondered if Robbie was in that last set. He had remarked about whether the war was worth the bloodshed when he'd come back from the confederation conference. Now was probably not the right time to ask, though.

"What I am saying, Vihansa, is that no one is going to hold your name against ye. 'Tis your actions that count."

It didn't seem she was going to win her argument with this thread. Time to change topics to a well-worn trope. "I do not have anything to wear." She stifled a smile at her unexpected pun and the fact that sounded more like something Charlotte would put in one of her novels.

Anne waved a hand in the air. "Ye can find a gown in Inverness when ye go in with Cook. Several shops have ready-mades."

"But I've no coin for that."

"We have accounts at all of them."

"Shopping takes time, though. Cook will want to get the food back here as soon as possible."

"Hmmm. I suppose ye are right about that." She contemplated for a moment and then smiled. "I'll have Robbie escort ye, then."

"*No*!" Vi realized that had come out a bit loudly and lowered her voice. "I mean... Men do not like to go shopping with women."

Anne broke into a grin. "I ken. 'Twill teach him a lesson for having stopped your fencing practice earlier." She picked up the papers on the desk. "And I'll nae hear any excuses from either of ye."

Vi suddenly felt like she'd swallowed lead. A shopping trip with Robbie? It was a disaster waiting to happen.

****

This trip was a disaster. Robbie trudged behind Vihansa, trying to balance numerous oddly wrapped packages, none of which fit together in any kind of bundle. A pet octopus would have been handy right now, if one were trainable. Or—had he thought of it sooner—a couple of stable lads who could have served as footmen on this shopping expedition.

Instead, he had looked over the lot of them suspiciously when they left that morning, still trying to determine which one had lent trews to Vihansa. His common sense had finally come to the fore when he realized that Jamie was far too tall for his trews to have fit that tightly on her. So here he was, trotting after her like a pack mule, while she stopped in front of yet another store.

"Ye are going in this one too, I suppose?"

She gave him a contemplative look. "I haven't finished purchasing everything on the list."

The list. The one he'd love to grab, rip into pieces, and toss to the wind. Anne had shown it to him before she'd given it to Vihansa. In addition to the gown and slippers Vihansa was supposed to purchase for the ceilidh, Anne had included several day dresses, bonnets, half-boots, and a number of undergarments that had put him in the uncomfortable position of trying, unsuccessfully, not to notice while they were laid out and then of trying to curb the mental image of Vihansa wearing them. He suspected his cousin had deliberately detailed those items—down to the color and amount of lace—and was no doubt laughing at him from home.

"So what do ye need from this shop?" he asked, trying to hold the door open and not drop any of the packages. Vi grabbed one that was slipping and put it on top of the rest. At least, she hadn't expected him to grow a third hand to take it.

"A negligee."

Robbie bit back a groan. Now he'd have to purge another mental image of her.

"Anne said to make sure it was silk."

Lucifer's horns! Had his cousin conferred with the devil himself to make up that list? He was almost assured that she had when the shopkeeper held up a garment that was all but transparent. It would hide none of Vihansa's curves or anatomy.

She was frowning. "I don't think that's what Anne had in mind."

He was pretty sure that was *exactly* what his cousin had in mind. They were going to have a long talk when he got back.

Vihansa fingered the material. "This would hardly be warm."

It would if she were lying next to him with his arms wrapped around her. He cursed silently as he pushed the thought from his mind. The conversation with Anne was going to be a very, very long one.

"I think I'll pass."

"No." The word was out before he could stop it. The image of her wearing it hadn't completely disappeared, although he wasn't about to let Vihansa know where his thoughts lay. *Lay* maybe not the best word to use at the moment since his groin was stirring. "If 'tis on my cousin's list, ye'd best get it." The last thing he wanted was to have to accompany Vihansa on another shopping trip involving intimate apparel. "I am sure she has a reason for it."

"I hadn't thought about that." Her brows drew together. "She is probably wanting to have this available if her husband has the chance to visit her."

Robbie almost laughed. Angus would care nothing

about silk lingerie if he had a chance to visit. Neither would Anne. No. He knew what this—and the other undergarment purchases—were for. His cousin meant to punish him for halting the fencing lesson that day. However, he nodded sagely. "'Twould be a good reason."

She nodded and smiled at the shopkeeper, then added the wrapped parcel to his stack a few minutes later.

"Are we ready to go home now?" he asked when they were out on the sidewalk.

Vihansa gave him a look that a headmistress at a school might use with a very slow student. "We still have to find my gown for the ceilidh."

He bit back another groan and managed to keep from looking around to see if a being sprouting horns wasn't lurking behind some post. The devil had to be following him, because he didn't think this day would ever end.

Chapter Six

The shopping trip with Robbie had been somewhat enjoyable after all. Vi had to admit it was rather fun to load him down with packages and lead him about from one shop to another for hours because the best part was, *he couldn't complain*. Anne had made it quite clear he was doing penance. She had even gone so far as to imply that there would be a second—longer—shopping expedition if she found out he'd been grumbling about it. It had been quite satisfying to watch the thunderclouds roll across his face as he kept quiet.

Of course, Karma had come early, and this evening at the ceilidh she was paying for her behavior. At dinner, she'd taken a random seat only to have two quite elderly men claim the seats on either side of her. Neither of them had lost any time in informing her that he was looking for a bride and each had boastfully claimed that she should choose himself. Unfortunately, they were both hard of hearing, so their intentions were loudly proclaimed for all within shouting distance to hear. Anne was seated at the head table on the dais, too far away to notice. Robbie was somewhere in the crowded hall...most likely in the middle of a bevy of women at the far end, she suspected. Not that she'd expect him to come to the rescue. She was hardly a damsel in distress. She could handle these would-be suitors.

"Ye'll have the first dance with me," the one named

Duff said.

"Och, nae!" the other one, Brock, countered. "The lassie has promised it to me."

Vi kept her voice low. "I've not promised anything."

"Aye, there! Ye see!" Duff shouted. "The lass has chosen me!"

"'Tis nae what she said," Brock nearly bellowed.

"Ye ken ye trip over yer own feet," Duff hollered back. "The lass is wise to say nae to ye."

"She didna say nae!" Brock roared.

"*Gentlemen.*" If there was ever a euphemism, that was it. They had attracted the attention of at least two dozen people around them. Some were openly gawking, others were concealing laughs behind snickers, and a few were regarding her with the solemnity of a jury about to go into deliberation.

It was the last group that concerned her. She had no idea to which clans Duff and Brock belonged, but she was a Sutherland in their midst. The only name worse would have been Campbell. She couldn't afford to insult anyone.

"Gentlemen," she said again. "I am afraid I will not be able to dance with either of you. I turned my ankle this afternoon." She gave each of them a smile that would have made Charlotte happy to use in one of her novels. "It pains me to walk, let alone try to dance. I'm sure you understand."

They both looked somewhat mollified and some nodding and throat-clearing was done before Duff said, "Aye, lass. I'll sit with ye then." Duff gave Brock a little smirk.

Brock glared back at Duff. "As will I. We'll see whose company the lass prefers."

Vi bit back a groan. Just like Robbie hadn't been able to complain about the shopping trip, she wasn't able to complain about these circumstances either.

Karma had definitely paid her a visit.

****

Once the dancing began, Robbie was swamped with requests to dance. He'd always been popular with the lasses, partly because he really enjoyed dancing. This year, he was even more in demand since so many of the men had gone to join the prince's forces. He was looking forward to dancing with Vihansa once his obligation to the local lasses was done.

He'd spotted her sitting on a bench near the dais, flanked by the two old cronies Duff and Brock Macpherson. They'd fought together in the 1715 Uprising and were forever trying to best each other in the telling of it. His instinct had been to go to her and find out if she needed an escape, since the discussions often turned into heated arguments, but since Angus was away, his responsibility was to play host. Then he'd noted an odd thing happening. Several younger men had ventured over—he was keeping a list of those in his head—but she'd refused to dance with any of them. It was odd the sense of relief he felt in that, but obviously, she wasn't in need of rescue. So he'd turned his attention to who was next in line to dance.

Anne approached him during a short interval when the musicians were taking a break. "I think 'tis safe to say the ceilidh is a success."

"Aye." He looked around at the flushed faces of the young women. "I'd say some of them will be needin' new dancing slippers."

"No doubt in part thanks to ye," Anne replied.

"Ye've been quite busy on the floor. How many times did Janet and Morag manage to snag ye?"

They were the lasses who'd come up to him at Hogmanay and to whom he'd promised the first two dances. He shrugged. "Three each, I think."

His cousin raised a brow. "'Tis good ye are nae in London. I hear if a man dances with a girl three times in one night they are all but betrothed."

He grimaced a little. The two of them were competitive and each had clutched and clung once the music was done. "I have nae intention of going to London."

"A ball and chain can be attached here too, ye ken," Anne said.

He grinned at her. "Doona fash. I have nae intention of letting that happen." He was well aware of the feminine wiles the lasses played on him with their flirting. His grin slowly faded. There was definitely one woman who didn't flirt with him. At all.

"I've noticed Vihansa is nae dancing this eve."

Anne nodded. "Someone told me she said she'd turned her ankle this afternoon and it would hurt to dance."

Well, that explained her refusing the other men. He furrowed his brow. That didn't mean she didn't *want* to dance. Maybe Duff and Brock had attached themselves to her because she was—more or less—a sitting duck. Maybe she really did need rescuing from those two. It had been a couple of hours—and he'd noticed them beside her at dinner too. How much of their conversation could she take?

He looked over the heads of the crowd as it began to take positions for the next reel, but when he could see the bench she'd been sitting on, she was gone.

And so were Duff and Brock. His frown deepened. Where had they gone?

****

The problem, Vi thought, with weaving a lie was that somehow the web always got entangled, to paraphrase Sir Walter Scott. She had thought feigning a turned ankle would cleverly get her out of dancing with Duff and Brock while sparing their feelings, and they'd soon be off to find other prospects.

No such luck. Instead, they'd followed her—each taking one of her elbows to support her "weak" ankle that had her practically levitating off the floor to the bench where they promptly seated themselves on either side. When she'd suggested there was no need to stay with her and that they should enjoy the evening, they'd been noncommittal and promptly started arguing over who should fetch her a glass of water and who should stay behind. Apparently each thought the other might persuade her to marry him whilst alone. She'd clearly forgotten how acceptable such an arrangement was in the eighteenth century.

Having a "sore" ankle precluded her from accepting a dance invitation from anyone else, and she sighed, resigning herself to the situation. Web-weaving was obviously not her forte. When Duff's and Brock's conversation eventually turned to who might be reiving their sheep and who should have been responsible for watching over them in the first place, she shifted her attention and promptly saw Robbie dancing with one of the girls who'd been flirting with him at Hogmanay. Morag, she thought her name was. The girl was buxom, with raven hair that swirled around her shoulders as she moved, managing somehow, to brush against Robbie when others were well apart. He laughed and spun her about before the couples moved and exchanged partners. This time it was the other girl, Janet, who managed to press herself close, her hands running across his chest before the music had them switching partners again. This time it was a girl Vi didn't know, but she was all smiles and wide-eyed looks before another took her place, smiling seductively and mouthing something to Robbie before she moved on.

It was probably an invitation to meet somewhere later—although, Vi thought sardonically, she might have to wait her turn since it seemed Robbie was singularly sought out by every female who could walk. From the way all those women surrounded him between reels, he must have been convincingly agreeable to their wishes.

She frowned. Robbie reminded her of Matt.

"Ye doona look like ye are having a good time, lass," Duff said.

She startled, having been lost in thought, and shrugged. "It is a little boring to just sit."

Brock glared at Duff. "Ye oaf! Ye've made us ignore the lass with our talk."

"I didna start talking about sheep, ye eejit," Duff shot back.

"*Gentlemen.*" Vi forced a smile before the two of them would be off on another row. "It is not your company that is lacking. It's just..." She floundered for a moment. "It's just that my ankle is paining me. Perhaps you would excuse me? I'd like to go to my room."

"Aye," they both said in unison and rose together as if the move had been choreographed. "We will see ye there."

"No, there's really no need." She started to rise, but found herself being lifted and suspended in the air.

"I willna let ye walk on that ankle," Duff said.

Brock puffed up. "And I, personally, will nae allow ye to further damage it."

A strange feeling bubbled up her throat, much like a hysterical giggle. Charlotte would be having a field day with this scenario, but all Vi could think of was that her tangled web was just getting worse.

Chapter Seven

"Cumberland has arrived in Edinburgh."

Anne made the announcement the next morning as they were sitting down to break their fast. Robbie had a bannock halfway to his mouth and laid it down as the others in the morning room off the kitchens halted their actions as well, to stare at her. Only Vihansa didn't seem overly surprised.

"When?" someone asked.

"Why?" asked another.

"He got there two days ago, according to the messenger…" She gestured to the man who was sitting at the table. "As to the why, ye might ask him."

The man nodded. "I suspect King George is finally realizing the seriousness of Prince Charles's revolt."

Robbie nodded. "He must be. Cumberland was supposed to be preparing London for a French invasion."

"Which isn't going to happen."

All eyes pivoted to Vihansa after she spoke.

"How do ye ken that?" Robbie asked.

Her eyes widened and she turned pink. "I…I meant, it *probably* wouldn't happen."

Robbie frowned slightly. Her tone had sounded very confident when she'd originally said it *wouldn't* happen. Had her Sutherland kin known something?

"The French have sent munitions and coin to support the Cause," Robbie said, "and there were French soldiers at Falkirk. What makes ye think more help is nae arriving?"

Vihansa looked decidedly uncomfortable, which wasn't like her at all.

"It…It's just a theory I have."

"Ye have a theory about war, lass?" The messenger gave her an owlish look. "Ye are a woman."

Since he was sitting next to the man, Robbie got prepared to duck should Vihansa decide to throw a dish or goblet at the eejit.

"Let's hear your theory." Anne let her gaze linger on the messenger long enough for him to understand her unspoken message and then glanced at the other half-dozen people at the table. "We will hold your confidence, Vihansa, if ye are fashing about that."

Vihansa nodded, still looking somewhat wary. "Since Britain was the strongest opponent to France gaining ground in the Austrian Succession War, it made sense for King Louis to support Prince Charles and create a diversion in Scotland. It worked because King George had his son—Cumberland—return from Flanders to guard London, and France gained more territory." She looked around the table as if assessing whether she should continue. "My theory is that King Louis doesn't feel he needs to expend any more resources to help the prince now."

There was a momentary silence following her statement, and then the messenger spoke again.

"How do ye ken so much about what is happening on the warfront? 'Tis nae natural for a woman."

Robbie shifted his chair out of missile range from whatever table weapon Vihansa might choose to use and wondered how such a dimwitted fool could be trusted to be a messenger. Surprisingly, though, Vihansa just smiled at the man. *Smile* might not exactly describe her expression, Robbie reflected, but her lips were pulled back from her teeth. He half-expected a feral sound to emerge, but her voice was calm when she answered.

"Before I became orphaned and came to Scotland, I spent time in both Austria and Prussia. There was already unrest there because Charles—the Holy Roman Emperor, not Prince Charles—had no Habsburg male heirs. His daughter, Maria Theresa, would eventually reign *suo jure.* " She paused, giving the messenger a hard look. "Given most males' opinion of women's ability to lead, war was pretty much predetermined."

Robbie stifled a laugh.

"That does make sense," Anne said. "Since King George's attention has been diverted, King Louis has nae need to keep supporting our cause. He can now concentrate on gaining more ground in the Succession war. Prince Charles should be notified." Anne smoothed her napkin on her lap. "I believe I'll invite him to come to Moy Hall."

That statement drew more astonished silence, and then everyone started talking at once. It wasn't until later, after Anne and Vihansa had left, that Robbie realized he hadn't been able to question her about where the hell she and the MacPherson men had gone last night. And, he suddenly thought, she hadn't been limping this morning, either.

****

Vihansa almost tripped on Anne's hem as she quickly followed her out of the breakfast room. The last thing she wanted to do was loiter and be asked more questions by Robbie. She wouldn't have slipped and made that remark about the French not planning to intervene any longer if she hadn't been so blasted distracted by him.

She'd spent most of last night—after managing to persuade Duff and Brock that they *didn't* need to see her any further than the door to her room—sitting by the window, looking out over a moonlit landscape. She'd seen the silhouette of a couple and wondered if he was out there strolling with one of the many women who had practically formed an eighteenth-century fan club. She didn't even know why it was important if he were. She had learned her lesson with Matt—to keep her distance from charismatic men who surrounded themselves with women. Not that Robbie had made any attempt to come over and ask her to dance. *That* vexed her too, and she didn't know why. She gave herself an inward shake and switched off the unsettling thoughts.

"Do you think the prince will really come here?" Vi asked Anne once they were in the study going over the many lists of things that needed to be done.

"I am nae sure," Anne replied, "but Alexander mentioned in his last letter that the prince needed a rest."

Alexander MacGillivray would be the relative who led the troops she'd raised for the prince. Vi chewed her lip pensively. He would also be killed at Culloden unless she could somehow manipulate the outcome of that battle. The opportunity to actually meet Prince Charlie might be her big chance to do that.

"The prince is at Bannockburn. Do you think he'd travel this far north just to rest?"

"I got the impression from the letter that, even though we had a victory at Falkirk, the prince is not that pleased with the confusion of the outcome. Alexander said a fair number of troops scattered because they thought we had lost. Scouts have been sent out to bring them back." Anne smiled. "It would probably be better that they don't have to face the prince immediately on their return."

"That would probably be wise," Vi replied. "but do you have the resources to protect him while he's here? So many able-bodied men are off fighting."

"Doona fash about that. The prince always travels with his own protection. Besides, although Alexander was careful nae to be too specific in the letter, I think the prince intends to attack the fort at Inverness and rout Lord Loudoun. As close as we are, he could use Moy Hall for a base."

"You think he'll bring hundreds of men, then?"

Anne shrugged. "It could be a thousand or more since Colonel Campbell has at least two thousand soldiers at the fort."

"How in the world would you feed that many men? Your servants will run themselves ragged."

"Well, if need be, I can contact Angus' mother in Inverness to send some of her servants to help."

Vi felt her eyes widen. "You're on good terms with her, even though her son is fighting for the government?"

"Och, aye. 'Tis nae reason for us to be enemies."

"I wish more people felt like that. The world would be a better place."

Anne nodded. "It would be, but we canna change that. We can only fight for what we believe in, even if it means separating families sometimes."

Vi nodded too. It really wasn't so different from the Civil War in the States when brother sometimes fought brother. "Still, it must be hard for you."

"It is. I'll nae deny it." Anne sighed. "'Tis why Robbie doesna want to take sides."

"I have wondered about that."

"His mother was a Sassenach. Robbie was just a bairn when his da was killed fighting in the '15. His mother tried to return to England with him, but she was waylaid by highwaymen."

"English?"

"We doona ken. 'Twas my da who found her body in a ditch, with Robbie wrapped in a blanket by her side, nearly dead too." Anne paused. "So, my cousin is half-English and half-Scottish, which puts him in a quandary he'd rather not be in."

It put Vi in a quandary too. Her opinion of Robbie was rapidly changing. His story was stirring memories in her that had been long buried. She was an orphan as well.

Only her story hadn't turned out quite like his.

****

Several hours later, Vi watched as Anne carefully spooned a bit of hot wax on the missive for the prince and then pressed the Mackintosh seal on it. She blew on it carefully and then sat back.

"We can wait for that to dry, then go to lunch."

It was amazing that the whole morning had gone by. They'd spent most of it listing all the myriad details that would need to be attended to if the prince accepted the invitation to visit. *When* was probably a better word than *if*, considering that Anne had told her Charles had been most appreciative of her sending him troops. It seemed there was a great deal of respect between the two of them. Vi only hoped she could instill a sense of respect for herself when she met him so she could plant a seed for a different strategy than history gave for Culloden.

Anne shoved her chair back and stood. 'Ready to get something to eat?"

Vi nodded and followed her down the hall toward the kitchen. Since there were so few of them in residence, meals were usually gotten directly from the kitchen rather than going to the Great Hall and having them served. As they passed the room where they'd had breakfast, the most wonderful smell wafted from it. Vi sniffed appreciatively.

"Cook must have made scones this morning. They're Robbie's favorite," Anne said as she sniffed too. "Let's see what kind she made."

As they went through the door, Vi stopped abruptly, almost colliding with Anne, and stared. At least a half-dozen baskets of scones of different varieties filled the round table and, sitting there, scooping clotted cream on one, was Robbie. She hoped he wouldn't bring up the conversation from earlier.

"Did Cook do all this?" Anne asked, taking a chair.

Robbie shook his head, chewed and swallowed. "Nae. 'Tis gifts."

Anne gave him an inquisitive look. "Gifts?"

"From last night's…er…guests."

Something about the way he hesitated before he finished the sentence made the hair at Vi's nape prickle. Evidently Anne was puzzled as well, since her brow furrowed.

"Why would any of our evening's guests bring scones over this morning?"

"Ummm…" Robbie shrugged and reached for a jar of jam. "I might have mentioned they are my favorite."

Anne's frown deepened. "To whom?"

Vi's nape hair practically stood up. She didn't need

to hear the answer to that. She *knew*. Robbie had been encircled by at least a half-dozen women when she'd left the dance last night, Morag and Janet among them. And there were a *half-dozen* baskets on the table.

He gave his cousin an affable smile. "Just a few lasses."

Anne shook her head. "Ye are incorrigible."

Vi couldn't have agreed more. Six women had spent their morning baking scones for him, no doubt in hopes of captivating him. Maybe they all had ambitions of becoming his bride, too. What was that old adage about the way to a man's heart? Briefly she wondered if any of them had run into each other, since the scones were all still warm.

She sighed. He was obviously used to having women cater to him. She couldn't even accuse him—not that it was her business—of intentionally leading the women on. He was a natural charmer, much like Matt had been. She hated to admit it, even to herself, that she was attracted to the man as well. *But*. Men like them were incapable of being satisfied with just one woman. She had learned that lesson.

She would do well to remember it.

Chapter Eight

A fortnight later, Anne received a reply just as they were finishing the noon meal. Robbie and Vi followed her to the study, where she broke the seal. Scanning the letter, she smiled.

"I take it the prince accepted your invitation?" Vi asked.

"Aye, but there's more." She gave a contented sigh.

Robbie shook his head when his cousin paused for effect. Although she wasn't given to dramatics, she was quite skilled in capturing and holding attention. It was part of what made her so persuasive in recruiting troops—first for Angus, then for Charlie. By the time she revealed her real intention, everyone was riveted and ready to agree.

"So are ye planning on telling us what has ye looking like the cat who just found the creamery door open?"

"I am savoring the moment." She held up the paper. "A few days ago, Major General Gordon forced the surrender of government troops at Ruthven Barracks."

Robbie whistled. The barracks were only thirty miles from Moy Hall. "'Tis quite an accomplishment."

"Aye," Anne went on. "Charles is leading half the army here—"

"Here? He's bringing hundreds of men here?" Robbie interrupted. "How soon?"

Anne held up a hand to stop him. "Doona fash. They'll be bringing the artillery along, so that will slow down the regular soldiers a few more days."

"What about the other half of the army?" Vi asked. "Are they going to stay at Stirling?"

"Nae. They've abandoned the siege." Anne glanced at the letter again. "It doesna say here, but I *think* Charles plans to rout John Campbell from Inverness."

Vi looked askance. "Do you think the Earl of Loudoun will actually leave?"

"It depends. General Murray is leading the other half—mainly Lowlanders—via Montrose and Aberdeen. Again, I *think* the idea is not to alert the earl that the entire army is approaching. Surprise is always a key element."

"It will be for us if all those regiments land here," Robbie muttered.

"We're in a good position for them to camp here and rest. Far enough away from Inverness nae to be spotted, yet close enough to be fresh to attack." Anne replied. "The important thing is to get the government forces out of Inverness. It will be a huge gain for the Cause."

Robbie pointed to the letter. "Does it say when the prince might arrive?"

"Aye." She glanced down. "He's at Ruthven right now and plans to stay three days to make sure things are settled."

"When was that message sent?" Vi asked.

"The rider left yesterday…" Anne's voice trailed off and her eyes widened. "Good heavens! That means Charles will be here the day after tomorrow."

"'Tis short notice." Robbie shrugged. "I hope he's nae expecting a royal welcome."

"Charles Stuart is going to be the next king of Scotland. Of course he's going to get a royal welcome." She looked at Vihansa and shook her head, indicating that he, Robbie, was clearly an eejit.

Vi grinned. "I guess we need to get busy then."

****

It had been a whirlwind of activity and Vi hadn't gotten more than a few hours' sleep, but they had managed to get Moy Hall ready for the prince's visit.

Charles had arrived late in the afternoon with only an entourage of fifty accompanying him. As part of the receiving line, she'd been briefly introduced to him. The history books depicted him as looking boyish and radiating charm, but in spite of an easy smile and effusive manner—no doubt cultivated at the French court—under the shock of red hair, she'd seen the hard look of determination in his eyes. The prince might be young, but he was also resolute in his mission.

"I think you've accomplished somewhat of a miracle," she said to Anne as they stood at one end of the Great Hall viewing the guests milling about after the banquet that evening.

"*We* accomplished it," Anne replied. "I doubt I could have done everything if I hadn't had your help. But aye, 'tis a miracle!"

Vi hoped another miracle would happen the next day. Anne, and Robbie most likely, planned to meet with the prince privately to discuss his plans for attacking Inverness. She'd asked Anne if she could accompany them since the prince might wish to have information regarding the flight of the Sutherlands after Dunrobin Castle had been taken. Of course, the information would be what she'd gleaned from twenty-first-century history books, but it would still be accurate. Anne had agreed that she would ask. Robbie had looked like he wanted to argue the point but had actually held his peace.

"I still question the wisdom of nae having a dance tonight," Anne said.

Vi shook her head. "I think you made the right decision. Everyone is eager to talk to the prince. If there were dancing, he'd be obligated to participate in each reel. Every woman would want to dance with him and the ones that could not be fitted in would feel insulted."

"I suppose ye are right about that." Anne looked over the crowd surrounding the prince. "'Tis more important that Charles be available to converse and build support."

Just like any twenty-first-century politician, Vi thought. At least she wouldn't have to stand around watching Robbie dance with those six women who'd baked him scones. She tried not to feel too guilty for suggesting there be no dance. Several of them were hovering near the prince at the moment, and she looked around for Robbie. She finally spotted him near the main entrance to the hall, immersed in conversation with yet *another* woman. She had beautiful auburn hair flowing loosely around her shoulders. She looked vaguely familiar, but Vi was sure she hadn't seen her at the ceilidh.

"Do you know who Robbie is talking to?" she asked Anne.

Anne squinted, then shook her head. "I've nae seen her before. Mayhap she's with the entourage."

Vi supposed that was possible, although she hadn't noticed any women—not even camp followers—arrive with the prince's retinue. Before she could dwell on it, she heard two familiar voices behind her. Taking a deep breath, she turned around and forced a smile. "How are you this evening?"

"I am feeling braw!" Duff announced loudly.

"Nae more fit than me!" Brock said equally vehemently.

"That is good to hear," Vi said politely and looked over her shoulder toward where Robbie stood. The attractive woman was gone. For some unknown reason, she breathed a sigh of relief.

"'Tis good of ye to say, lass, because we—Brock and I—made a decision."

She smiled again, trying to ignore the near-deafening sound. "And that is, gentlemen?"

"That ye will choose between us tonight," Brock trumpeted.

Her smile faltered. "I beg your pardon?"

"Nae need to beg, lassie!" Duff grinned boisterously. "I ken ye'll choose me to be your husband."

"Nae if she has any sense." Brock scowled at his friend. "I'll be the one to marry her."

"If ye are still alive." Duff glared back and then looked at Vihansa. "I'll call him out at dawn if ye doona make a choice."

Vi stared at both of them, wondering if she were having some kind of hallucination. She'd stepped through a time portal, so maybe this was another kind of time warp? She'd have laughed if they both hadn't look so deadly serious. She felt like she'd swallowed lead. In the eighteenth century, a marriage could be decreed by royalty, just like that, and the prince was in attendance. It *could* happen. Tonight. She turned to Anne, but her friend had disappeared. Vi was alone.

For the first time in her life, she thought she might faint. She took a deep breath, hoping to clear the lightheadedness. "I think I need to sit down."

****

Robbie had just made his way over to talk to the prince when Anne tugged hard at his sleeve. He furrowed his brows at the agitated look on her face, which was unlike her. His cousin was always calm and steady.

"What is it? What's wrong?"

"Vihansa."

"Vihansa?" Robbie looked across the room. She was sitting on a bench between the two MacPhersons. "What's she done?"

"Nothing. It's just that…" Anne sounded flustered. "Something does needs to be done, though."

"About what?" This was so unlike Anne that Robbie was becoming unnerved as well.

"Is something amiss, my lady?" Prince Charlie asked from behind him.

Anne shook her head. "'Tis nothing to concern yourself with, my lord. We…have a bit of an argument going on."

"Is Vihansa arguing with the MacPhersons?" Robbie looked over to where they still sat. Vihansa was sitting still as a statue.

"Who is Vihansa?" the prince asked.

"She's the lady sitting over there." Anne gestured. "Robbie rescued her on Hogmanay." Briefly, she explained the situation, then turned back to Robbie. "Duff and Brock are insisting she choose one of them to marry or they are going to call each other out at dawn."

"*What*?"

"Since you rescued the lady, perhaps you should

intervene," the prince said mildly.

"Aye." Robbie turned on his heel and stomped across the room. It was no secret that the two MacPhersons were highly competitive with each other—they fought over everything—nor was it any secret that they both wanted a young wife. But how had they settled on Vihansa? What had happened on the night they'd disappeared during the ceilidh? Well, he'd figure that out later. Right now he had to remove her from the situation. Forcing a smile, he approached the bench and nodded to the MacPhersons.

"If ye'll excuse me, I need to have a word with Vihansa."

Duff's expression turned mulish. "We are having a discussion of our own."

"Aye," Brock agreed with him for once.

Robbie managed to keep his smile in place, although it felt frozen. "It's verra important that I speak with her *now*."

"Nae until we have an answer from her." Brock said stubbornly. "She has to choose which one of us to marry."

"I cannot." Vihansa suddenly sprang up, as though coming out of a stupor. "I cannot marry either of you."

"Why nae?" Both of them spoke in unison.

"Because…because…"

For once, Vihansa seemed at a total loss for words and she was white as newly fallen snow. Instinctively, Robbie put an arm around her and drew her close before she could swoon. To his surprise, her arm curled around his waist and she actually clung to him.

"I can't marry either of you because…" Vihansa drew a trembling breath. "…because I want to marry

Robbie."

Stunned, he himself nearly staggered at her words. He quickly schooled his features, hoping his shock wouldn't show. He must not have heard correctly. She wanted to *marry* him? They mostly argued. Why...? Then he looked into her eyes and saw the silent imploration there. Of course. By saying he wanted to marry her too, the MacPhersons would save face. It was a good solution. What harm could it do? The MacPhersons would be leaving soon. He nodded to both men.

"Aye. I want to marry the lass as well."

"Splendid!" Prince Charlie clapped his hands. "A hand-fasting to celebrate an end to a wonderful banquet!"

Robbie froze. When had the prince come up behind him? Robbie had been so engrossed in what he would say, he hadn't noticed. He felt Vihansa go rigid against his side. Slowly, he turned.

At least a dozen people stood with the prince, grinning widely and, following the prince's words, started to applaud. The noise drew the attention of others in the room, who started to flock over to see what the commotion was about. In no time, the message was being passed around. Hand-fasting. Betrothal. Marriage.

Anne stood silently, apart from the others, giving them a thoughtful look.

"Well, now," the prince said jovially, "let's seal this event and celebrate with a kiss." He turned to the people behind him. "What say you?"

They roared their approval and pressed close. Beside him, Vihansa had gone as still as stone. Now what in Hades was he supposed to do? He certainly wouldn't *mind* kissing her. Truth be told, he'd thought of it often enough. She had the kind of mouth that begged for kissing—generously wide, with full, sensuous, soft lips. He'd even thought about silencing her with a deep kiss when they fought and how that could turn a heated argument into a different kind of heat. But he'd never kissed a lass against her will. Meanwhile, the crowd was beginning to hoot.

He lifted a hand to caress her cheek with one finger and then leaned close to whisper in her ear. "'Twill satisfy Brock and Duff if we do this, but I'll nae force ye. 'Tis your decision."

He felt her hesitation and was about to drop his hand when he felt her body begin to relax. Slowly, her hands crept up his chest and her arms entwined around his neck as she lifted her face to his. He needed no further invitation.

He bent his head, his lips brushing against hers gently as he cradled her head in his palms. Feeling no resistance, he pressed more firmly, angling his head for a better position, reveling in the soft resilience as her mouth moved against his. His tongue lightly stroked the crease of her lips, and she gasped. More than anything, he wanted to take advantage of that and thrust his tongue fully into her mouth to taste her, but he restrained himself. Slowly, he ended the kiss and straightened.

She looked flustered and he felt a swell of pride. Even if she had allowed him the kiss only to be done with this awkward situation, he'd still gotten *some* reaction from her.

Charles grinned at them and raised a glass that someone had given him. "To the happy couple!"

****

To the happy couple, indeed, Vi thought a couple of hours later when the crowd had finally gone home and the prince with his entourage had retired for the night. She had just finished helping Anne and the kitchen staff clean up, and it was the first real moment she'd had to think about what had happened.

She wasn't quite sure what had gotten into her that she'd *said* she wanted to marry Robbie. Desperation, probably, since Duff and Brock had been deadly serious about her choosing one of them. Her declaration had been a means of escape and it *had* been successful. Tomorrow, she'd explain to Robbie that she had no plans to hold him to any hand-fasting announcement. The MacPhersons had already left, and once the prince was gone, there'd be no more talk of it. No harm done.

The kissing was quite another matter. She'd understood the need for it, but she hadn't expected her body to respond. Maybe it had been the very gentle caress to her cheek or maybe that Robbie had left the choice up to her, but once his lips had touched hers, emotion had taken over logic. Her breasts had suddenly felt heavy and full. Heat had pooled between her thighs. *And* she'd wanted to continue the kiss. It was a good thing Robbie had drawn back when he did or she'd have made a fool of herself—or, to put it in terms of the eighteenth century, she would have been behaving like a brazen hussy. That would have given Charlotte something to write about and Athena something to chortle over.

She shook her head at such foolishness and picked up the last trays from the table and carried it to the kitchen. She'd just come back out when she heard a banging on the front door. It was close to midnight.

Maybe one of the guests had forgotten something? She saw Anne walking toward the front door and decided to follow her in case she needed some kind of help.

A lad, barely old enough to shave, practically fell through the door when Anne opened it. He was panting heavily as if he had run a long way.

"Lachlan?" she asked. "What are ye doing here at this hour?"

"Lady Mackintosh needed to warn ye," he said between gulps of breath, "that Colonel Loudoun is marching to Moy with his entire army." He gasped more air. "They intend to take Prince Charles captive."

Chapter Nine

Vi stared at the youth, then turned to Anne questioningly.

"Lachlan works in my mother-in-law's household," Anne said by way of explanation and then turned back to him. "How do ye ken this?"

"The lassie who works at The Horns pub overheard Colonel Loudoun talking to his men earlier. They somehow found out that the prince was coming to pay ye a visit." He breathed easier now. "Ye've nae much time."

"Aye." A grim look of determination crossed Anne's face. "Ye go out to the stables and rouse the blacksmith. Tell him to bring the stable lads here." She glanced at Vi. "Ye go get Robbie while I wake the prince."

Before Vi could answer, she and Lachlan were both gone. Robbie's room was in the family wing of the house, opposite the guest quarters where hers was. As she made her way up the stairs she realized she'd not been in this part of the house and had no idea which room was his. She tentatively knocked on two doors before he opened the third one. For a moment, she just gaped.

He was shirtless. From his smooth pectorals across his broad chest to his heavily muscles biceps and his completely flat abs, he was sculpted like a Greek statue. A bronzed version of one.

He raised an eyebrow inquisitively, a half-smile on

his lips. "Are ye wanting to consummate the hand-fasting, lass?"

"What?" His question brought her to her senses. Did he think she was taking that nonsense seriously? "Of course not. Do you think I would…" She stopped, remembering *why* she was here. "Anne needs you. Loudoun and his army are descending on Moy Hall."

The smirk left his face. "Now?"

"Yes. They found out about the prince. We just got warned…" She stopped speaking again because Robbie had grabbed a shirt and was already running down the hallway to the stairs.

By the time they got downstairs, the place resembled a madhouse. The prince, looking somewhat sleepy and sloppily dressed, waited impatiently while his men scattered to saddle their horses. As soon as the prince's was brought to the door, he left, fleeing into the woods. His retinue would not be far behind him.

Meanwhile, Anne was in deep conversation with the blacksmith, the four stable lads and Robbie huddled around them. Vi could hear only snatches of conversation, but she could see lots of nods and grunts that she assumed were approval for the plans they were making.

In just a few moments, the small group disappeared into the night, leaving her and Anne in the foyer with the sound of sudden silence. Anne handed her one of the swords that were kept propped against the wall and took another.

"And now we wait," she said.

****

"So Loudoun turned back?" Anne asked the next morning as Robbie sat at the breakfast table, devouring a large plate of ham and eggs.

"Nae only turned back," he replied as he reached for a warm bannock. "The entire army didn't bother with Fort George and were headed toward Sutherland, the last we heard."

All eyes turned to Vi at the mention of her surname. Robbie almost wished he hadn't mentioned it. Not surprising that he had, though, since seeing her this morning brought back vivid details of her arriving at his room last night. For the first brief moment when he'd opened the door, he'd actually thought maybe she *did* have copulation in mind. There'd certainly been *something* akin to lust in her eyes as she'd looked at him. His manhood had started to rise to the occasion. Then she broke the news, and whatever momentary madness had overtaken him disappeared in a heartbeat. The idea of Vihansa visiting his room for licentious purposes was sheer lunacy on his part. Still, the less anyone associated her with the government-leaning Sutherlands, the better.

Robbie nodded at Donald Fraser. "Ye need to tell them how we routed Loudoun. 'Tis a good story."

The blacksmith grinned. "Aye. We went about two miles down the road to the narrow pass at Craig an Eoin. The lads helped us set up stacks of turf divots and peat that we could hide behind and wait—"

"Those hillocks we made looked like men in the moonlight too," Jamie interrupted. "'Twas a smart idea ye had, Lady Mackintosh."

"It's *Colonel* Mackintosh now," Vi corrected him gently. "The prince gave her the rank."

Jamie's eyes widened. "'Tis deserving it is. And ye, Vihansa…did he give ye rank too?"

Robbie frowned. When had Vihansa given Jamie

leave to call her by her Christian name? The lad had a bit too much gall. Vihansa didn't seem the least insulted, though, and gave him a genuine smile.

"Of course not, Jamie."

"Mayhap we can let Donald continue?" He tried to keep the irritation out of his voice.

"Och, aye," the blacksmith continued, "we could hear them coming, but we waited until they were close enough to hear us. Then Robbie and I sprang out and started shouting commands for the MacDonalds and Camerons to form the right and left flanks while "we" took the middle—"

"And the rest of us fired muskets and banged swords on rocks as we moved quickly from place to place so Loudoun would think there were hundreds of us," Jamie said.

Robbie tried not to glare at the lad, which was especially hard after Vihansa told him how impressed she was.

"Would ye let your uncle finish?" he nearly growled.

Jamie looked crestfallen and Vihansa gave Robbie an annoyed look, which didn't help. "Sorry, lad," he muttered.

The blacksmith shrugged. "'Tis nae too much more to be said. Loudoun most likely thought the rest of Prince Charlie's army had arrived and it was all of them attacking him instead of just the handful of us."

"And they turned tail and ran," Jamie said, although he gave Robbie a wary look.

"You should be proud," Vihansa said. "It was brave and very well done of you." She looked at each of them. "I wish I could have been there."

Robbie startled. "A woman has nae—"

"No place on a battlefield," she finished the sentence for him. "I am well aware of what you think a woman's place is."

Not *what*. *Where* would be more appropriate as the image of her standing in front of his bedroom door last night emerged in his mind once more. Judging from the challenging look she gave him, it might be wise not to express that particular thought. Still, it might be interesting to spar with her on the subject…

With a sigh, he reached for another bannock to stuff into his mouth before he could change his mind.

****

This particular incident would be forever recorded in history, Vi thought, as she went about helping Anne tidy up the remnants of the mess left behind when the prince and his men had escaped last night. It gave her a real thrill that she had actually been able to experience it, although she was disappointed that she would no longer have a chance to talk to the prince and try to convince him to listen to his elder, more experienced generals.

"I hope the prince hears of Loudoun's retreat and advances on Inverness," Anne said sometime later as they finally finished with the cleanup.

"I suspect he will," Vi answered. "It's an opportune time, since Loudoun's retreat must have left Fort George woefully undermanned."

A pensive look came over Anne's face. "I wish I kenned if Angus was still at Fort George or if he was with Loudoun's troops."

Vi heard the wistful tone in her voice. "Do you miss him, then?"

"There are many times that I do. In spite of our age

difference, he respected me."

"Even when you disagreed with him?"

Anne smiled. "I think *particularly* when I disagreed with him."

"So he enjoyed arguing with you?"

"In a way." Anne shrugged. "Sometimes, when I hear you and Robbie in a row, I think of him."

Vi laughed. "I doubt Robbie would compare our arguments to yours and Angus's, especially since we are not married and you are."

"Ummm. Speaking of that…" Anne hesitated.

Vi was pretty sure what Anne was thinking. "If you're worried that I took last night's declaration of hand-fasting seriously, you need not be. Robbie simply allowed both Brock and Duff to keep their pride intact by agreeing to marry me. He knows I didn't mean it and I know he didn't either."

"Be that as it may…" Anne hesitated again.

"What?" The hair at her nape began to prickle.

Anne sighed. "There is the fact that the prince declared ye hand-fasted."

"He was just caught up in the spirit of the moment." The prickling grew sharper. "He's gone now anyway."

"Everyone heard the declaration." Anne gave her a sideways glance. "More importantly, Duff and Brock heard it."

"They've left too." Vi tried to squelch her rapidly rising wariness. "Everyone can just go on their merry way as though nothing happened."

"But something did." A sympathetic expression crossed her face. "Ye ken, in Scotland 'tis the same a betrothal, although either of ye can break the bond after a year and a day."

"A year…" She stopped and looked at Anne. "You aren't suggesting that Robbie and I actually *act* like we're hand-fasted, are you?"

"Nae *act*." She paused. "Ye *are*."

"We can't be."

"Ye *can*. If the MacPhersons catch wind that all was a ruse, we would be risking clan war. The prince needs all of us." Anne shook her head. "We canna battle amongst ourselves. Nae now."

"But…" Vi grasped for a straw. "Robbie would never agree to this!"

"He already has." Anne's voice was gentle, but firm. "Your things have been moved to his room."

Vi tried to speak, but no words came out. Her vision blurred as the world around her tilted dangerously to one side and then to the other. From a far distance she heard Anne asking if she was all right. She would have laughed at the question if she could remember how. Of course she wasn't all right. For all she knew, she might quite well be mad as the proverbial hatter. Maybe she was living in a delusion of her own making and not in the eighteenth century at all… Maybe…

Her head slowly cleared and so did her vision. Sound and speech returned. Anne was still standing beside her, a worried expression on her face. So. This was reality, then.

Vi took a deep breath. Apparently, Culloden wasn't the only battle she was going to have to fight.

Chapter Ten

Robbie stood in the hallway outside his bedroom door later—very much later—that evening, wondering what the hell he was going to do. Before he left this morning to rendezvous with General Murray, Anne had taken him aside and explained the "facts" of the situation. Charles had—in front of everyone present—declared Vihansa and himself hand-fasted and no one was going to argue with the prince, let alone insult the MacPhersons. When he'd said Vihansa would never agree to it, his cousin reminded him that it was *her* idea. That was true—he remembered his own stunned reaction to her words—but he'd quickly realized it was simply a way to get out of an awkward situation. Now, it was even more awkward. Vihansa was on the other side of the door to his bedroom.

He had no idea what to expect. He'd spent the entire day with Murray, the other Jacobite leaders O'Sullivan and Drummond, as well as the prince, trying to decide on a strategy to lay siege to Fort George, which was still occupied by the English Major Grant and a regiment of men who hadn't been with Loudoun on the Moy defeat. Mostly, instead of deciding on a specific plan, the men Robbie had been with squabbled amongst themselves and he'd not been able to get a definitive report for Anne.

He didn't want to brook another argument, at least not tonight. He'd waited until past midnight to return home. Anne, not surprisingly, had been waiting up for him, although he wasn't sure if it was because she wanted a report or to inform him that Vihansa had moved into his room. When he'd asked if Vihansa had willingly agreed to that condition, his cousin had merely shrugged and said Vihansa understood.

Whatever the hell that meant.

He supposed there was a slim possibility that Vihansa hadn't protested the idea. His manhood hardened at the thought. Vihansa was a beautiful woman and, in spite of their sparring—or maybe because of it— he found her independent spirit challenging. He smiled. There were definite *advantages* to being hand-fasted. They would be expected to act as husband and wife for at least a year and a day, after which they could each decide to be free. Meanwhile they could—with all honor and respect—share the enjoyment of all sorts of bed-sport. Having her warm, soft, naked body curled up to his every night…

His smile turned into a grimace. That option had about as much probability as King George handing over the throne to Charles.

He shook his head. Here he was, holding his boots in one hand and standing like a complete fool out in the hall pondering what to do. God in heaven. If anyone came by and saw him, seemingly as undecided as a green lad in front of *his* bedroom, he'd be the laughingstock of the whole hall by morning.

At least he could be thankful there were very few occupants in this wing and the servants had—he hoped— retired for the night.

He hoped Vihansa had as well, since the hour was late. If she were fast asleep in his bed—the image made his groin stir again and he pushed the thought firmly away—he could use the settee tucked into a corner. It normally served as a tossing place for his clothes. It would do for the night, and they could discuss the logistics of their situation in the morning. Taking a deep breath, he opened the door quietly and stepped inside.

"I've been wondering when you'd get here."

He almost tripped over his own feet. Vihansa was sitting in the leather armchair by the hearth that was crackling with a new log. Not only was she fully dressed, she was also holding a fire poker. She wasn't smiling either.

He sighed. So much for postponing a discussion until morning.

****

When Robbie came through the door, Vi maintained her best *I'm the teacher* face that she used on freshman students, although she was tempted to laugh out loud. He'd been standing outside that door for a good fifteen minutes. She'd heard shuffling—probably when he was taking his boots off—and then other slight noises that made her realize she wasn't alone.

"Would ye mind putting that poker down?"

"I might." She'd picked it up when she first heard movement, since the door didn't have a lock. Then, when no one tried the doorknob, she'd settled in the chair and waited. "Then again, maybe not. You gave me quite a fright, standing out there."

He eyed her warily. "Ye doona look frightened."

She shrugged. "I've been told it's not good to show fear."

"True enough." He set his boots down but didn't move from his location by the door. "But I swear ye'll nae have to fear me. Ever."

That was rather a nice, chivalric thing to say. After all, she wasn't opposed to *chivalry*, only chauvinism. With a sigh, she laid the poker on the floor beside her. "I will take you on your word, then."

"Ye have my word." He grinned. "But even if ye didna, kenning that ye can probably swing an ax, wield a sword, and…" He pointed to the poker. "…use that as a weapon would make me keep my distance from ye."

Well. *That* wasn't exactly something a knight-in-shining-armor would say. Not that she was looking for a knight, in armor or otherwise. She'd always been proud of her self-defense skills. Women needed to be able to take care of themselves. Still, that he'd practically said he'd *avoid* her…

She frowned. Wasn't that what she wanted? Wasn't that why she was fully dressed? Why was she confused? She was usually a clear, logical thinker and now she was feeling…hurt? Which was silly. She should be relieved that Robbie had all but said he wasn't going to pursue consummation of the hand-fasting. She had a sudden strong urge to glance toward the big four-poster bed that would easily hold two. No. No…*No*.

"You might as well come inside." She managed a smile. "I think the room is large enough to allow the distance you want."

An odd expression crossed his face. He opened his mouth to speak, then snapped it shut as he made his way over to the chair opposite hers by the hearth, sank into it, and closed his eyes. "'Tis a long day, lass. I'd rather nae argue tonight, if ye doona mind."

For the first time, she noticed how tired he looked. Anne had told her he'd gone to meet with Murray,

Drummond, O'Sullivan, and the prince. From the history accounts she'd read, the first three of them were all strong-willed and used to being in command, and she'd seen the determination in the prince herself. It could not have been an easy day trying to get them to agree. And, even if Robbie didn't know it, having them all reach an agreement was crucial if the battle at Culloden was to have a different outcome. An idea clicked in her mind.

Maybe Fate had given her a good hand to play with this hand-fasting business. She'd have Robbie's ear often enough if they were to spend every night in this room. Maybe she could persuade him to convince the prince to listen to Murray. But that was something she could dwell on later.

"I agree. No arguing tonight," she said. "I'll sleep on the settee for tonight so you can take the bed and have a good rest."

When he didn't answer, she shook her head and got up. Had she expected him to play the knight again and insist she take the bed? Good grief. She was getting as sappy in her thinking as one of Charlotte's heroines in her romance novels. This was Robbie's room, after all, and it really wasn't his decision that she was here anymore than it was hers.

But as she settled herself onto the settee, she heard a soft snore. She looked across the room to the empty bed and then saw that he had fallen asleep in the chair, his feet propped up on an ottoman.

For a moment, she was tempted to wake him, then decided against it. When she was that tired, it would take a major earthquake to make her stir, and she wouldn't appreciate it.

She'd be okay on the settee, and if he woke, he'd see

the bed waiting for him.

And tomorrow, they would settle this whole ridiculous thing.

****

Dawn was breaking, sending pale lavender beams of light through the window, when Robbie opened his eyes. For a moment, only half-awake, he wondered why he'd been sleeping in a chair. Then he remembered. Vihansa.

He sat up quickly, ignoring stiff and sore muscles that protested the fast movement, and looked at the bed. It was empty. Not only empty, but the covers were immaculately in place. It had not been slept in. Had she slipped out after he'd fallen asleep?

He heard a faint sound from the far corner of the room and glanced toward the settee. Something stirred, a blanket lifted, and then the bundle muttered what sounded like a curse. Seconds later, Vihansa's head popped out and she sat up, rubbing her shoulder.

"I doona think either of us had a comfortable night."

Vihansa blinked and looked around as though trying to place where she was. Then her gaze returned to him. "Why didn't you take the bed?"

"I only just woke up." He tilted his head toward her. "Why did ye nae take the bed?"

"Because it's *yours*."

"But I was obviously nae in it." He gave her a quizzical look. "Ye doona think I would take advantage of ye in your sleep, do ye?"

Her brow furrowed before she shook her head. "No, but that's not the point. It's your bed. This is *your* room."

He lifted a brow. "I think 'tis *our* room now."

"Nonsense."

She tossed off the blanket and he saw that she had

stayed fully dressed, which was probably just as well, since seeing her sleeping in a shift in *his* bed would have given way to all sorts of stirring thoughts that he doubted she'd share.

"I wouldn't be here if I hadn't said what I did and the prince hadn't overheard it and made that announcement," she continued.

"But he did make it."

"Yes, yes. I know. Anne explained how we had to pretend to go along with it—"

"Pretend?"

"Yes. Just so no one would be offended." She stretched to one side and then the other. "But today is a new day. The prince has moved on. He'll be focusing on taking Fort George and probably not even remember—"

"What makes ye think Charles's plan is to lay siege to Fort George?"

She looked nonplussed for a moment, before she shrugged. "Wasn't that what you were meeting about yesterday?"

"Aye." He wondered if he'd been talking in his sleep.

"Anyway, I doubt the prince will remember or care." She waved a dismissive hand. "The MacPhersons are safely home now, so I'll just tell Anne you and I had a big argument last night—which will be easy to believe—and we called the hand-fasting off. I can move back to my room today."

"It doesna work that way." He folded his arms and waited for the explosion.

She stared at him. "Why not? You didn't want this arrangement either."

He ignored that and the thunderclouds building

across her face. "We took a vow."

"We did not! Neither you nor I actually agreed—"

"We did, lass." He wouldn't be surprised if lightning bolts flashed from her eyes next, but he had to finish. "Even though we spoke no words, we sealed the vow with a kiss." He recalled that kiss perfectly—and how she'd reacted to it—although this was probably not the best time to remind her. "It canna be undone for a year and a day."

"A *year* and a day living like this?" She gestured to the settee and the chair. "You cannot be serious."

"Well, nae actually. Two days have gone by, so 'tis only three hundred and sixty- four more." He smiled, hoping to defuse the situation before the brewing storm broke.

Her eyes narrowed. "You think this is funny?"

Tread carefully, laddie. His uncle used to tell him that when he was about to make a monumental mistake.

He stopped smiling and shook his head. "I doona see any humor at all. 'Tis just…"

He took a deep breath. If Vihansa was going to unleash her wrath, so be it. "I am a Scot. A Farquharson. My clan—and the Mackintoshs—would disown me if I didna live up to my word."

The explosion he'd expected didn't come. Instead, Vihansa went still and stared into space. She was quiet for so long he was beginning to wonder if a physician needed to be called.

"Are ye all right, lass?"

She blinked, as though coming back to reality from wherever she had been. Finally, she nodded and gave a deep sigh.

"I suppose I can get used to sleeping on the settee."

"Nae. Ye will take the bed."

"You can't keep sleeping in the chair." She frowned. "You cannot take the settee either. You won't fit."

He paused. "The bed…'tis big enough for both of us."

Both eyebrows rose. "Are you proposing that we be hand-fasted for real and consummate this farce?"

If he'd held out any fantastical hope that maybe they *would*, it was obvious with her words that they would *not*. It was his turn to sigh, although he tried not to let it show.

"As I said, the bed is big enough for both of us with room to spare." He pointed to the blanket she'd used. "I'll get a couple more of those and create a bedroll to place in the middle, and we'll each stay to our side." He took a deep breath and looked at her. "And ye have my word—as a Scot, as a Farquharson—I'll nae lay a hand on ye."

****

Vi was still thinking about those words as she went down to break her fast. Robbie had turned on his heel and left the room immediately after that, giving her no time to respond. Not that it probably mattered.

She'd lain awake most of the night considering options. She understood Anne's point. She'd even agreed—more or less—to play out the role, at least for the night. While she was waiting for Robbie to show, she'd weighed other possibilities and come to the conclusion that if they mutually agreed it had all been a mistake, the matter would go away, just like the prince and the MacPhersons had. The idea of continuing this charade for a year was unthinkable. Then again, if she couldn't prevent or change the outcome of the battle at

Culloden, Robbie might not be here in two short months.

That idea stopped her cold on the staircase.

Robbie could be one of the fifteen hundred Jacobites who would lose their lives that fateful day. A chill swept through her. She didn't want anything bad to happen to him, even though, as contradictory as it seemed, she considered him bossy and a ladies' man to boot.

But was Robbie a ladies' man? He had the same knack for attracting women that Matt had...and even Matt hadn't had six women bake scones for him after a party. But was that Robbie's fault? Matt had been a philanderer and craved attention from women. Did Robbie?

Vi snorted indelicately as she continued down the steps. It didn't matter if Robbie did or didn't. He'd given his word that he wasn't going to lay a hand on her. Unlike Matt, Vi sensed that Robbie spoke the truth. Even if they shared the same bed, he'd keep his distance from her. He'd already made that clear earlier.

She paused as she reached the bottom of the stairs. Maybe it had been easy for him to make that vow because he didn't find her attractive. Surprisingly, the idea stung a little. She was female, after all. Robbie probably saw her as a weapon-wielding woman who wore pants and didn't respond to being told what to do. Unlike the women who baked him scones.

Well, so be it. Vi lifted her chin and walked toward the kitchen. She didn't care anyway.

Chapter Eleven

Anne and Vi had just finished archery practice when Robbie galloped into the courtyard, spraying gravel and raising dust as he reined in and hopped off his horse before it had come to a complete stop. It was a feat any Texas cowboy would have been proud of and, from the grin on Robbie's face, he was too.

"I take it ye have good news?" Anne asked as he came over to them.

"Aye. Major Grant surrendered Fort George this morning."

"Without bloodshed?" Vi asked.

He nodded. "Nae wounded, either."

"I want to hear how *that* came about," Anne said.

"Let me get a pint of ale first, and I'll tell ye."

A short time later, they were settled in Anne's study. Vi watched Robbie covertly. Since their pseudo-hand-fasting arrangement a few days ago, he'd been making himself scarce. He left early in the mornings, presumably to meet with the prince and his generals since the Jacobite army was now at Inverness—he stood in for Anne who, as a woman, couldn't take part in strategizing discussions—and came home well after dark. He'd then confer with Anne in her study until late into the night. Vi always pretended to be asleep when he finally got to his room—she still thought of it as *his*—so she'd not had a chance to question what progress had been made.

"Could you start at the beginning, please? Don't leave out any details, either," she said and then added, "I'd like to know how you managed to take the fort without casualties."

"As would I," Anne said.

"Well," Robbie began, "O'Sullivan carried out reconnaissance two nights ago and told the prince the army wouldn't be able to breach the double walls."

"Did the prince argue the point?" Vi asked.

"For once, nae." Robbie shrugged. "Probably because O'Sullivan already had another plan in mind."

"Which was?"

"He noticed that, while the walls were strong, the foundation facing the bridge was unstable. He suggested building an emplacement on the hill across from it, placing a cannon there, and blasting the bastion out from under the bridge in the morning." Robbie leaned back in his chair, looking pleased. "It worked. With nae a way for the English to escape and the Jacobites surrounding him, the major decided it best to surrender."

"That was wise of him," Vi said. "I am glad the prince followed his advice."

"Perhaps," Anne responded pensively. "I mean, 'tis good no one was killed or hurt, but Cumberland willna be happy he didna stand his ground."

Vi glanced at Anne and then turned to Robbie. "He shouldn't be coming—I mean, do you think he'll come here himself?" Good Lord! She'd almost made a huge gaffe.

"If he does, he willna have a fort to stay in." Robbie grinned. "After all the provisions had been taken out, the prince ordered the walls razed and the bastions blown up so the English canna claim it again."

Vi nodded. "Robert the Bruce did the same."

Robbie gave her a quizzical look and she realized she'd almost made another *faux pas*. Apart from definitely not supposed to be knowing—from twenty-first-century history lessons—that Cumberland wouldn't come to Inverness, women weren't supposed to be historical scholars in *this* century. "My father liked to tell stories of the *other* fight for Scottish independence."

Anne smiled. "Let's just hope that we are victorious this time too."

Vi nodded her agreement, but she knew it was going to take more than hope to change the outcome at Culloden.

*****

As Anne finished the notes she'd been taking during their conversation, Robbie had time to study Vihansa. She intrigued him, even if she was one of the strangest women he'd ever met. She was skilled with various weapons, the latest of which appeared to be archery. She seemed to know history well, even though Prince Charlie hadn't had the success at Stirling and Bannockburn that Robert Bruce did. Interesting, too, even though she'd changed it into a question, she'd sounded so confident with her comment about Cumberland not advancing to Inverness, almost as if she knew the future. Which, of course, she couldn't. She simply had a keen interest in what progress had been made and also in *how*. He'd never known a woman who was actually interested in war strategies.

But, he had to admit, Vihansa intrigued him in other ways too. It was sheer torture going to their room each night, knowing she would be sharing his bed but he couldn't touch her. He'd deliberately delayed going there until he was pretty sure she would be asleep. Even so, as soon as he quietly slipped into his side, his manhood stood to attention, ready and eager to do what a man and woman were *supposed* to do in a bed.

Which is what his member was starting to do again right now. Thankfully, Anne interrupted the beginnings of his fantasy.

"I'm going to go put these notes in the safe in the secured room," she said. "Then I'll meet ye for the midday meal."

As they stood to follow her, he frowned. He hadn't noticed before, intent as he was on delivering his message, but Vihansa was wearing men's trews again today that left little to the imagination. And his imagination had already been playing havoc with his mind. He didn't need any very real, physical reminders of just how alluring she was.

"I thought ye were supposed to be getting a riding habit like Anne's," he all but growled.

One brow lifted slightly. "I have one."

"Then why are ye nae wearing it?"

"I have always thought that a riding habit is for *riding*." Her tone was one that might be used with a child that was none too bright.

"It has other uses," he said stubbornly.

"Indeed." She smiled in a convivial manner.

"Anne wears one." he muttered, sounding somewhat like a petulant child, even to himself. "She's wearing one now."

"I prefer wearing trews. They're more comfortable."

"They show off too much of ye."

She stared at him for a long moment, then shook her head. "In case you haven't noticed, besides yourself,

Donald and the stable lads are the only men around here, and they've shown me nothing but respect."

"I doona like it."

Her eyebrow went up. "Are you telling me what I can wear?"

"We are hand-fasted, ye ken."

Her brow went higher. "In name only."

Her voice was deceptively calm, which should have been a warning, but he couldn't seem to help himself. He didn't want other men looking at her in those form-fitting trews, even if they acted respectful. He jutted his chin. "Still."

Vihansa's temper seemed to snap. "Where I come from, women are allowed to choose what they want to wear, and I will continue to do so."

Before he could respond, she spun on her heel and left the room, leaving him gaping. When had the Sutherlands started letting their women wear trews?

****

As soon as the words were out, Vihansa wished she could take them back. Since she couldn't, she did the next best thing and fled the room. Hopefully, Robbie wouldn't read too much into the *where I come from* part.

It certainly seemed to be her day for misspeaking. Not about wearing pants—she fully intended to keep doing just that—but she'd almost given herself away three times in just a short time. If she kept making inane remarks, they'd think her mad and probably lock her away somewhere. She was going to have to be continuously on her guard if she were going to be of any help at all.

Robbie was already seated at the table by the time she got to the dining room. Anne was there as well, thank goodness, and, even better judging from the looks on their faces, they were involved in a serious discussion of some sort. She should be safe from any further questions Robbie might have.

"I think ye should use your influence on the prince," Robbie told Anne as Vi sat down.

She frowned. "What influence? The prince has already thanked me for gathering troops for him. Unless I can round up another score or two—"

"He calls ye *La Belle Rebelle*...the beautiful rebel," Robbie interrupted. "He doesna do that to others."

Anne smirked at him. "Maybe because I'm the only female in his army?"

"I think Robbie has a point," Vi said, "even though I don't know what he wants you to influence Prince Charlie about. He did seem to be somewhat smitten with you during the short time he was here."

Anne waved a dismissive hand. "He's spent too much time at the French court, probably taking lessons from King Louis on how to make every lady feel special."

"I suspect the archduchess of Austria might disagree with you, considering France is trying to repudiate her claim to the throne. And, since the prince wants French support, he wouldn't flirt with Maria Theresa, either." Vi smiled widely. "So his paying special attention to you—"

"Nae special." Anne shook her head. "In any event, I'm hardly in the same league as a Holy Roman Empress."

"The Austrian succession issue aside," Robbie said, "the prince does seem willing to listen to ye, which I canna say he does with Murray, O'Sullivan, or

Drummond."

Anne gave him a sharp look. "What do you mean?"

Robbie sighed. "I've spent the last few days in heated discussion with all of them. 'Tis all they do, argue."

Vi gave him a contemplative look. She'd thought he'd been staying away because he was avoiding sharing his room with her as much as he could. Had all those long days and even longer nights away from Moy Hall been legitimate?

"What do they argue about?" Anne asked.

"Och, Drummond is still annoyed that O'Sullivan got credit for the surrender of Fort George—"

"Good heavens," Vi cut in. "It's done and over. Can they not agree to move on? There are more important issues ahead, like—" She stopped abruptly. She'd almost said too much *again*. "I mean…Cumberland is already in Edinburgh. They may have to deal with him next…" When Robbie gave her an intense look she added, "Well, it could be a possibility." Dear Lord, she hated to sound so weak. To her surprise, Robbie nodded.

"Ye are right. The main problem, though, is between the prince and Murray. The prince doesna like deferring to him."

"Even though the general is twice his age with more than twice his experience," Vi couldn't help but say, even though it drew a thoughtful look from Robbie. Scotland was going to lose the battle at Culloden unless the prince started taking the advice of his leadership. "Can you not persuade him to at least consider General Murray's strategies?"

"'Tis hard to tell a prince what to do," Robbie answered and then turned to Anne. "Which is why I think ye could be of great influence, cousin. He will nae take offense at your suggestions."

Anne gave him a questioning look. "I can hardly invade his council at Inverness. If ye think his officers canna agree amongst themselves, imagine the turmoil I would cause, stepping over them?"

"True," Robbie agreed, "but ye can host a gathering in celebration of the falling of Fort George and Loudoun's retreat."

"Hmmm." Anne grew pensive, then turned to Vi. "What do ye think about that idea?"

Vi paused. Prince Charlie probably wouldn't listen to her either since she was a stranger, and a Sutherland at that. But, if Anne could influence him, then *she*, in turn, could feed her ideas to Anne.

"I think Robbie's idea is a good one," she said and forced a smile. She wasn't looking forward to another ceilidh, but that was of little consequence considering time was running short. Something needed to be done.

Anne grew thoughtful once more and then finally nodded. "I'll do it."

Vivian sighed inwardly. If that meant having to watch Robbie's six-woman fan club flock around him again, then so be it.

Chapter Twelve

About the only thing the prince and his command staff had agreed on this morning was that the idea of ceilidh at Moy Hall was a good one. When Robbie arrived earlier, O'Sullivan and Drummond were being barely civil to each other, Murray's face was set like stone, and the prince was the next thing to petulant.

They were all now seated at a round table—which Robbie thought ironic, given that none of them were acting like the egalitarian knights of legend.

"Has there been any word on Loudoun?" he asked, hoping it was a benign question.

"Aye." O'Sullivan glanced at Drummond before continuing. "The last message I received is that he is reorganizing in Sutherland, along with one of the Black Watch regiments."

"And I heard that regiment is under Captain Mackintosh's command," Drummond added, although he didn't look at O'Sullivan.

Robbie wondered if Anne knew. She got letters from her husband, but Robbie doubted they contained any critical information, considering they were on opposing sides of this war. Anne hadn't shared anything, either, which he thought she would if it were pertinent to the prince.

"Isn't that woman staying with ye a Sutherland?" Murray asked.

"Aye," Robbie answered warily. "Why?"

Murray shrugged. "I'm just wondering what kind of connections she might have. William Sutherland was her guardian, was he not?"

"I believe the earl took her in after her parents died," Robbie answered.

"I'm also wondering why she didna follow him when Cromartie seized the castle."

"The earl escaped through the postern gate, if I recall," Robbie replied. "I doona think he considered taking the household with him."

"I would think a ward—especially a female one—would merit that consideration."

Robbie frowned. What was the general alluding to? "I canna answer that, but ye and I both ken womenfolk left behind are often considered spoils to be taken. 'Tis why Vihansa ran."

"Mayhap." Murray looked skeptical. "Or the earl could have instructed her to come here to seek shelter so she could gather information."

Robbie gave him an incredulous look. "Ye think Vihansa a spy?"

'It's a possibility. *Someone* let Loudoun know that the prince was advancing to Inverness."

"That could have been anyone." Robbie could hardly hold his anger back. "An entourage of even fifty men is nae exactly easy to hide."

"'Tis true." The prince gave Murray an abrasive look. "While I was at Moy Hall, I did not observe anything that would convince me that Vihansa Sutherland is a spy." He gestured to Robbie. "I would not have approved his hand-fasting to her if I did."

Murray's eyes widened slightly as he looked back at

Robbie. "Ye are hand-fasted to the woman?"

Robbie nodded since there wasn't anything he wished to actually say. Officially they were, even if, behind closed doors, nothing had taken place, but he could hardly point that out. He'd be laughed right out of the room for not taking advantage of what was—by Scottish law—rightfully his to have. Instead, he tried to avoid thinking of Vihansa at all, since every time he did—especially spending the night with her—his male parts started aching with need. He had agreed to act as Anne's envoy to these strategy meetings mainly because it would keep him away from her.

"Ye are sure she isna working her feminine wiles on ye?" Murray asked, apparently still not convinced. "Remember that Delilah was Samson's downfall."

Robbie managed to squelch a guffaw at the absurdity of Vihansa even flirting with him, let alone trying to use "feminine wiles" on him. She was one of the most straightforward, say-what-you-think persons he knew. Best to act a bit insulted, though, to stop Murray from more questioning.

"I've been around my share of lasses, ye ken." Robbie raised one brow. "Are ye saying I wouldna be smart enough to recognize such a thing?"

Murray didn't take the bait. "I'm saying it's possible that the Earl of Sutherland planted his ward in Anne Mackintosh's household to gather information."

He was beginning to understand why the prince didn't like taking orders from Murray. His own temper was beginning to simmer because the man was as persistent as a Highland terrier at a rabbit hole. He pushed away the thought that Vihansa *did* ask blunt questions sometimes and made remarks that seemed odd, as if she knew something the rest of them didn't, but was that unusual for a woman who could handle weapons almost as well as he could? She'd travelled in Prussia and Austria, so she had been aware of the Succession War on the Continent and the ongoing conflicts between England and France. None of that made her a spy.

"If ye doona believe me, ask Anne. She approves of the lady."

"And I trust Anne Mackintosh's judgment," the prince added.

Murray gave him a steady look. "I am aware that ye call her *La Belle Rebelle* and are quite fond of her."

The prince met his look. "Are ye accusing Colonel Mackintosh of using *her* feminine wiles on *me* as well?"

Murray's brows rose. "Colonel? Ye made it official?"

"Yes. She deserves the honor for sending me several hundred men, even if she cannot command the troops herself."

Robbie was tempted to intervene but restrained himself. Murray was venturing onto boggy ground by implying a personal interest between the prince and Anne. Admittedly, the prince was somewhat rakish, probably due to growing up in Rome and spending time at the French court. However, Anne had always been faithful to her husband, even given the present circumstances. She was as forthright and honest as anyone he knew. If he needed to defend her, he would, but Charles's announcement at least distracted Murray from pursuing more information about Vihansa. For now, that would do.

****

Once again, the Great Hall at Moy was full of

laughing people milling about after dinner, waiting for the trestle tables to be cleared and pushed back so the floor would accommodate dancing in a short while.

Vihansa stood to one side near the dais, watching the commotion, eventually spotting Robbie near the entrance. He'd finally put in an appearance late this afternoon and gone directly to speak with Anne. Since he'd been gone several days—and nights—the message was pretty clear that he was avoiding her. She sighed. Perhaps it was better that way, given their sleeping arrangements...which made *sleeping* difficult.

"I'd have thought ye wouldna be leaving Robbie out of your sight tonight."

Luckily, Vi had seen George Murray approach from her peripheral vision or she might have jumped out of her skin. She wondered why he would seek her out, since he was one of the guests of honor, but this might be an opportunity to make a subtle suggestion about Culloden, albeit a *very* subtle suggestion. She smiled at him.

"Actually, I can see Robbie from here." She gestured toward the other end of the hall where he and the prince were in a group that included the six women who'd baked scones for him. "He's quite engaged in conversation at the moment."

"Hmmm." Murray glanced over to the group. "I'd have thought ye'd want to be by his side since ye are hand-fasted."

She hoped her surprise didn't show as her breath quickened. She hadn't expected Robbie to acknowledge the pseudo-betrothal at all. "He told you that?"

"Charles did, actually."

Her breathing slowed. She should have known Robbie wouldn't go announcing something that wasn't even real. She supposed she'd have to keep up the façade, though, since the prince was in attendance too.

"It must have been quite an exciting evening for ye, what with the announcement *and* having Loudoun's troops marching this way the same night." Murray paused. "Come to think on it, Robbie mentioned ye handled that news quite well."

Vi frowned slightly. The general seemed to be hinting at something, but she wasn't quite sure what it was. "I'm not the sort of person to panic."

He gave her a thoughtful look. "That quality comes in quite useful at times."

The hair at her nape was beginning to prickle. What was he getting at? Maybe nothing. Maybe he was just a typical man, thinking all women were prone to the vapors in this century.

She lifted one shoulder in a half-shrug. "I find there's little value in overreacting and letting emotion rule over logic."

Murray studied her. "Was that a trait your guardian appreciated?"

Her guardian? What— Ah, yes. Her make-believe guardian, the Earl of Sutherland. She had no idea how he would actually feel. She shrugged again. "We never discussed it, since he had his hands quite full with what's been going on."

"If I were in his shoes, I'd find that quite useful."

She was beginning to feel irritated. "Instead of having to take care of another fragile female who might dissolve into tears at a wrong word directed toward her, you mean?" The words were out before she gave them thought, and she knew she should stop. George Murray was a general, and a lord as well, but... She forced herself to take a deep breath. He was also a *guest*. If she'd learned anything since stepping through a time portal into this world, it was that Highlander hospitality ruled over anything else. "That was...not necessary for me to say."

"Nae apology, though?" Something akin to a slight smile crossed his face. "I am beginning to think ye have a depth to ye that even most men doona have. I shall have to keep an eye on ye, I think."

She wasn't sure if he was giving her a compliment or a warning, but before she could answer, Robbie and the prince joined them. Murray bowed slightly and took his leave. As she watched him go, she realized she hadn't had a chance to give him a single suggestion regarding Culloden. It probably would have fallen on deaf ears anyway. She smiled at the prince. Maybe he would be more willing to listen.

****

Once Robbie saw that Murray was talking to Vihansa, he tried to break free of the group he was in and get over to her. Lord only knew what kind of an interrogation the general was putting her through.

It hadn't been that easy to do, though, since the prince was involved in the discussion and Robbie couldn't very well interrupt. He hadn't expected Charles to follow him once he'd broken away, but he did. Obviously, the conversations over the past few days had provoked the prince's curiosity as well.

"What were ye and Murray talking about?" Robbie asked, hoping he didn't sound too blunt. "Ye looked rather serious."

"We were discussing the success of the rout," Vihansa replied and turned to the prince. "Since I was in

Austria not too long ago, I observed events unfolding and was intrigued by the strategies that Prussia's King Frederick was using to try and oust the empress." She gave Charles a hesitant smile. "Do you think that strange?"

"Not at all, my lady. After all, *la belle rebelle* takes the same interest in my cause," the prince answered, "and I am very much aware of the situation in Austria myself."

'Of course. You were recently in France." She hesitated. "Do you share King Louis' feelings for repudiating the empress's claim to the throne?"

Robbie frowned, wondering where the conversation was going, and hoped Vihansa realized that Charles had recruited French support.

"Although the king allies himself with Prussia, Saxony, and Bavaria, his main concern is keeping the English off the Continent." The prince smiled widely. "I was the perfect pawn for him to get Cumberland recalled from Flanders."

"Do you play chess, then?" Vihansa asked.

Robbie blinked at the sudden change in direction and noticed the prince looked confused too, even though he nodded. "Chess? Are ye making a comparison of some sort?"

"Yes, I am," she answered Robbie and then turned back to the prince. "I think your describing yourself as a pawn is very accurate, since it is the first move made in the game. Of course," she added, "that move only sets the entire board into motion, which in this case means checkmating King George."

"Bravo!" The prince grinned again. "I like your analysis!"

"Thank you." She paused. "If you will allow it, I should very much like to sit in on any councils that include Anne or Robbie. I might be able to offer an opinion now and then to make sure you are the king to sit on Scotland's throne."

As the prince murmured his assent, Robbie had a strange feeling that the entire conversation—at least from Vihansa's standpoint—had an undercurrent as well.

He just didn't know where it was leading.

****

At least she'd gotten her proverbial foot in the door, Vi thought as O'Sullivan and Drummond claimed the prince's attention and led him off. She would now be privy to some of the strategy talks and, hopefully, could convince someone to persuade the prince to listen to the experience of the war-hardened officers and not rush into battle on the moor at Culloden. Maybe that auburn-haired girl Anne had thought was with the prince's entourage last time would be a good place to start. She squinted, trying to see across the room.

"Are ye looking for someone?" Robbie asked.

"Sort of. At the last ceilidh, there was a woman with reddish hair—"

"That describes a number of lasses in Scotland."

"I know that." Vi tsk-tsked at him. "Hers was different, though. More like a bright mahogany. Beautiful color. " She arched a brow. "So was she. You were talking to her."

He frowned, then smoothed his brow. "Ah. I think I remember the lass. She said her name was Bridgid."

Of course he'd remember her. What man wouldn't? And she was aptly named, too, for Bridgid had been a

Celtic goddess. The irony that they were both named after goddesses was interesting.

"Why do ye want to talk to her?"

"It might help to get to know her. Anne said she thought she'd come with the prince."

"She might have. She asked how I felt about the Colonies gaining independence at some point." Robbie shrugged. "Maybe the prince is thinking of helping them out once he's on the throne."

Vi bit her lip to keep from telling him that would happen sooner than he thought. "Well, I hope I see her later."

"I'll keep an eye out," Robbie replied. "Meanwhile, I'd like to ken something else."

'What?"

"Did Murray say something to upset ye while he was talking to ye?"

She kept her expression neutral. She had no real evidence that Murray had been leading up to anything. "Not really. Why?"

"Ye look like ye're deep in thought."

She managed a smile. "I was just thinking about the conversation with the prince. It's not every day I get a chance to talk to royalty."

Robbie didn't return it. "Ye looked serious before he said anything."

So he wasn't going to let her evade the question. She shrugged. "Murray asked a lot of questions."

Robbie gave her a sharp look. "What kind of questions?"

"Mainly about whether my guardian—the Earl of Sutherland—considered my ability not to panic an asset." She gave Robbie an arched look. "The general said you told him I had remained calm during the rout. That seemed to impress him for some reason."

"Did he ask ye about Sutherland?"

"Not specifically." The hair at her nape began to prickle again. "Why are *you* asking all these questions?"

Robbie hesitated, then took a deep breath. "Murray thinks ye may be a spy."

Vi's mouth dropped open, and she snapped it shut. A spy. The idea that anyone would think that hadn't occurred to her, but it probably should have. Sutherlands in this century were pro-government, not Jacobites, and she'd literally popped up at Hogmanay with a somewhat plausible excuse of escaping Cromartie's raid. It was her turn to take a deep breath.

"And what do you think?"

He shook his head. "I doona believe it."

An odd sense of relief washed over her. "Thank you. Please also believe that I would never do anything that would hurt either you or Anne. You've both been more than kind." Another thought hit her before Robbie could answer. "Did Murray tell the prince his thoughts?"

"The prince was sitting at the table when Murray spoke." Robbie gave her a half-smile. "I suppose 'tis good the prince and Murray are often at odds, since he didna agree with the general this time either."

That, too, was a relief to hear, although having just compared the Jacobite cause to a chess game—and the prince knew all the pieces in play—she would have to be careful what moves she made, particularly how she presented her opinions, to avoid being put in check herself.

The fiddlers struck up the first strains of their music just then, interrupting her thoughts. Folks began to pair up and head toward the middle of the now-cleared floor.

Robbie bowed in her direction. "Would ye do me the honor of the first dance?"

"Of course." She was almost tempted to curtsy, except that was an English custom, and she wasn't even sure how to execute a proper one. When he extended his arm, though, she nestled her hand in the crook of his elbow. Good heavens. Even through the coat and shirt Robbie wore she could feel the sinewy hardness of his forearm. It sent a little tingle through her. She wrapped her fingers a bit tighter, ignoring the glares from Morag and Janet as they passed by.

The opening dance was an exhilarating reel, and by the time it finished, people were flushed and a little breathless, but everyone clapped for more.

She turned to Robbie. "I suspect the ladies who provided you with your scones are all waiting for you to ask them to dance now."

He shook his head. "I willna be dancing with them tonight."

"Not with any of them?" She smiled at him. "Those scones couldn't have been that bad."

"'Tis nae the scones."

"What, then?"

He looked perplexed. "I am hand-fasted to ye."

"In name only. We haven't consummated anything."

Several expressions flashed across his face in succession. Surprise, then a scowl, followed by an intenseness that could have been—desire?—which was quickly squelched. It stirred an unfamiliar reaction in her, even though she'd probably imagined it. Now, though, a neutral expression befitting a professional poker player settled over his features.

"'Tis nae matter. I am hand-fasted to ye."

"But…but…" Her voice trailed off as guilt infused her. "It hardly is fair to you not to be able to dance with anyone else." She hated what she was about to say, but she had to offer. "Perhaps I should plead a headache and retire—"

"It wouldna matter."

"But…if I'm not here, no one would think anything of your socializing."

"'Tis nae importance what others think." He sighed, then gave her a direct look. "I made a vow to ye. As a man, 'tis important for me to keep it, even though we have the arrangement we do. Now—" He broke the intense gaze. "—I had better go play host to the prince."

She could only stare after him as he left, not sure her mind wasn't playing tricks on her. They had agreed to *act* as a couple to put an end to the MacPhersons' expectations and also not to defy the prince, but they both knew there was no intention of actually marrying at the end of the year-and-a-day. What man would willingly commit to a farce? What kind of a man would willing forego other relationships and be "faithful" to someone who slept with a huge tartan bedroll between them? She closed her eyes. An *honorable* man. That's who would do this. An honorable one. She'd obviously not met one before.

A hysterical bubble rose in her throat. She'd caught Matt in their bed with another woman shortly after they'd become engaged. Truly *engaged*. As in planning to get married.

She opened her eyes and looked around the room. People were laughing and talking. Another reel had started. Nothing had changed…except her perception of Robbie Farquharson.

Chapter Thirteen

"The prince is planning to march on Fort Augustus." Robbie burst into Anne's study with the news, two days after the ceilidh, having just returned from conferring with the command staff at the prince's temporary headquarters. He stopped abruptly when he noticed the sober expression on Anne's face and a similar one on Vihansa's.

"What is it? Is something wrong?"

Anne tapped a folded paper on her desk. "I received this message a short time ago. Cumberland is now in Aberdeen."

Robbie frowned. "He's moved north, then."

"I've told Anne that I think he's setting up base there for the rest of winter so he can gather forces and advance on Inverness in a few weeks," Vihansa said.

If he weren't so stunned about Cumberland's advance, he might have smiled. She certainly was taking her role as a "counselor" seriously. Before he'd left with the prince after the ceilidh, she'd told him she planned to become more involved. She'd even asked him to make Charles aware of the possibility that Loudoun and Sutherland might unite with Cumberland. Now, that recollection sobered him. He refused to consider that Murray might be right about Vihansa, but had that observation only been logical thinking on her part, or had she known something no one else did?

Vihansa gave him a thoughtful look. "Do you think it wise for the prince to be heading in the other direction right now?"

"Fort Augustus is the base for the English troops that have been raiding Cameron and MacDonald lands," he replied. "The lairds have asked Charles to put a stop to it since they're supporting his cause."

Vihansa grimaced. "Politics. It's the same everywhere."

"What?"

She started, then a wary expression settled on her face. "I…I just meant…people who have power always expect a favor in return. Like what the lairds are asking now."

He had a strange feeling that wasn't what she'd really meant, so he proceeded cautiously. "Land is everything to a Scot. Ye doona think they should ask for help?"

"I'm not saying they shouldn't. They have a right to expect their future king to support them." Vihansa shook her head. "I'm just thinking that the timing is not good, especially since Cumberland is much closer now than he was."

"As ye just said, 'tis doubtful he'll come to Inverness until spring," Robbie said, still cautious. "That will give the prince time to settle things for the Camerons and MacDonalds *and* gain him more soldiers once it's done."

"I see your logic," she answered, "but isn't surprising the enemy a key element to a successful battle?"

He frowned, not sure what she meant. "I doona think the soldiers at Fort Augustus are expecting the prince."

"I don't mean that fort." Vihansa studied him. "What about if the prince would march on Aberdeen? Now? In the middle of winter? If he could defeat Cumberland before spring, the war would be over."

"I doona think it would be that easy," Anne intervened and picked up the letter. "According to this, Cumberland brought five regiments of dragoons and sixteen of foot. They're currently housed in barracks."

Robbie whistled. Even he hadn't expected that many troops. "We would not only be outnumbered but our men would have to break through barriers while fending off both cavalry and foot. 'Tis better for the prince to choose a different battleground, closer to home—" He stopped as Vihansa jumped up from her chair, her eyes glistening suspiciously. Was she going to cry? He didn't think she wasn't the crying sort. Had he insulted her? "When the time for that battle comes," he said more gently. "And *if* it comes at all."

"Oh, it will. It will."

She brushed past him and ran out of the room. He could only gape in amazement because he thought he'd seen a tear trickle down her cheek.

****

She felt like a fool. Maybe she actually *was* a fool, for she'd run out of the house without a coat or even a shawl, but those items were in her—*Robbie's*—bedroom. The last thing she wanted right now was to take a chance of him following her and catching her crying.

She never cried. Not when she discovered Matt with his lover. Not when he left to live with her. Not even when she gave away the antique bedroom set she loved because she couldn't bear to sleep alone in the bed they'd shared.

But now, here she was, tears streaming down her face, threatening to turn into icy drops as she made her way to the stables where it would be warm. She knew what the outcome of Culloden would be if no one listened to her. Robbie might be one of the fifteen hundred Scots killed in a battle that would last only an hour. She didn't want to lose him like that.

The thought brought an abrupt end to her tears as she sank down into the straw of an empty stall. Dear Lord. Was she falling in love with him? She knew her feelings had changed since the night of the most recent ceilidh, when he declared he'd keep his oath and had asked nothing in return. He'd even kept his vow of not laying a hand on her. They'd gone to bed with the thick bedroll in place. So unlike Matt, who obviously couldn't keep his hands off any woman.

She frowned slightly as she realized that, for the first time, she felt no anger when recalling her ex-fiancé's promiscuous ways. The humiliation and betrayal of being cheated on was gone. If anything, she felt pity now for the other woman. He'd probably not be faithful to her either. But that would be their problem. She felt...nothing.

'What are ye doing out here, Vihansa?"

She blinked as Jamie entered the stall and knelt down beside her. "Did something happen? Are ye all right?"

"I'm...fine." She realized she meant it. She truly felt fine now. No more remorse. No more recalling the hurt of the past. She was finally through dwelling on it. She reached up to pat Jamie's cheek. "I'm fine."

"So this is where ye went."

Her hand froze as she looked up to see Robbie looming outside the stall.

****

Robbie just barely managed to restrain himself from hauling Jamie up by his collar and tossing him out of the stall. Or better, outside the barn. The smith's nephew appeared by Vihansa's side a little too often. Why was he here now? And why was she nestled in the straw? Robbie narrowed his eyes as he looked from her to Jamie.

"Get out."

Vihansa narrowed her eyes too. "He was only—"

"Get out." He clenched his fists.

Jamie eyed him warily, taking a step backward as he stood, putting himself out of punching range. "I thought she might be hurt."

He glanced at Vihansa. "Are ye hurt?"

"No, but—"

"Then get out," he said once more to Jamie.

Jamie backed away, his own fists clenched, and stepped out of the stall. Then, in defiance, he looked at Vihansa. "Ye call if ye need me."

Robbie waited for his footsteps to subside, although he didn't think Jamie had gone far. He took a deep breath and looked down at Vihansa. "Why are ye out here?"

"It's cold outside. I had to be somewhere."

He narrowed his eyes again. "Ye came out here to meet Jamie?"

"Don't be stupid."

"Stupid? Ye think I'm an eejit? I come out here to find ye lying in the straw—"

"I was not lying in—"

"Ye were clinging to Jamie—"

"I was not!"

Vihansa sprang to her feet with the agility of a cat. The sparks shooting from her eyes told him he might well take caution that she didn't claw him. "Nae clinging, then." He squared his shoulders. "But I saw him kneeling over ye, and ye were reaching out to him. Ye canna deny that."

She glared at him. "Jamie was concerned that something had happened to me. I was patting his cheek to reassure him that I was fine." She crossed her arms in front of her. "You can believe that or not."

He tried not to notice that her folded arms only raised the plumpness of her breasts. For a fleeting second, it seemed she was offering them to him. He shook his head. He really was an eejit.

She frowned. "You don't believe me?"

"What?" He looked at her in confusion, then realized he had shaken his head, which she took as an indication of his denial. He really needed to stop thinking about her breasts. "No—"

"Then there is no more I can say." She started past him.

"Wait." He caught her arm. "I didna mean I didna believe ye. I was thinking of something else." He looked around. Jamie was polishing a saddle not far away. Whether he meant to stay within range in case Vihansa "needed" him or whether he wanted to listen to the conversation, Robbie didn't know. He sighed.

"I think we should continue this conversation back at the house."

Vihansa glanced in Jamie's direction and then huffed at Robbie, "Fine."

He leaned down and picked up the shawl he'd

dropped. "I thought ye might want this."

For a moment, she stared at him, then she snatched the shawl out of his hands, swirled it around her shoulders, and silently stalked away, leaving him to follow.

Which he did at a more leisurely pace. Watching her hips sway as she stomped off was almost as intriguing as her arm-crossing had been.

****

By the time she reached Anne's study, Vi had sorted through some of her jumbled emotions and lost some of her indignation. It was rather hard to stay angry at a man who was thoughtful enough to bring her a shawl, even though he *was* a complete "eejit" if he thought there was anything going on between her and Jamie.

When Robbie finally entered the room—what had taken him so long?—she'd composed herself. When he closed and locked the door before taking a seat, she gave him a half-smile. "Are you going to lock me in until I make a confession?"

"Something like that." He glanced toward the door. "I don't want us to be disturbed until I have some answers."

Her smile faded. "Surely you don't think I arranged a tryst with Jamie? In broad daylight?"

His eyes narrowed. "But ye would at night?"

"Oh, for heaven's sake! *No*." A thought hit her and an odd little thrill flashed through her. "Are you *jealous*?"

"Nae." He lifted his chin. "But I willna be cuckolded."

"We are not married."

"We are hand-fasted," he said stubbornly.

"Good Lord! Is that what's bothering you? Appearances?" She suddenly felt deflated. Of course, appearances mattered, especially since the prince himself had decreed them betrothed. It was silly of her to think Robbie might be jealous. He was a proud Scot, and she knew what it felt like to discover a lover. She sighed. "I didn't mean to run into the stables. It was just so cold outside."

He frowned. "Why did ye run out in the first place?"

"Because you wouldn't listen to me."

"I listened." He looked confused. 'Anne told ye why marching on Aberdeen wasna practical."

"Yes." Vi paused. "She had a point, but you said it would be better to wait and pick a battlefield closer to home."

"Aye. 'Tis better to fight on familiar ground."

"True, but what if they choose a bad place to take a stand?"

"Doona fash about that." Robbie smiled at her. "Murray is a seasoned general. He'll choose a spot easy to defend."

"But what if the prince does not agree with him?" Lord, she had to make Robbie understand the importance of convincing Charlie to listen to Murray. "Can the general override him if need be?"

Robbie shook his head. "The general would not do that. Charles is the prince."

"But he's not commander-in-chief like in the States, is he?"

"'Twould nae be proper to overrule the prince." Robbie frowned suddenly. "What are the States?"

Her blood chilled. She'd made a huge blunder. The Revolution hadn't been fought yet. "I…I meant the

Colonies."

"In America?" His frown deepened. "How do ye ken they have a chief commander?"

"I...I just suppose they do." Best to change the subject and quickly. "Do you think you could persuade Prince Charles to take the advice of his generals?"

"I doona ken I have that much influence."

"But would you try?" Someone had to keep Charles from making the bad mistake that would cost Scotland everything. "Please?"

"I can try, lass, but I think ye are fashing too much. King George most likely sent Cumberland and those troops as a show of force and nothing will come of it."

"Cumberland is not simply rattling sabers. He's not going to just stay in Aberdeen."

Robbie eyed her. "How do ye ken that?"

Drat it. What could she say to convince him? "I doubt the king would send thousands of men to Aberdeen simply to make a statement. Cumberland will attack."

"Ye seem sure of that." Robbie studied her. "When we were talking earlier, ye said, 'He will, he will,' just before ye ran out." He closed his eyes, rubbed his forehead, then opened his eyes again and leaned forward. "Was Murray right about ye, lass? Have ye contacts with Sutherland? Is that how ye seem to ken what is going to happen?"

Vi froze, not sure how to respond. It was a logical assumption that she could be a spy, given her name and how she'd suddenly appeared out of nowhere. But if she went along with that story, Robbie would never trust that she had Scotland's interests at heart. Besides which, it would be a lie. So far, she'd managed not to actually lie, other than by omission perhaps. But could she tell Robbie the real truth? Could she trust *him* not to have her carted away to an asylum somewhere? It might be a chance she'd have to take since her present method of persuasion wasn't working. And *someone* had to stop Bonnie Prince Charlie from choosing to fight at Culloden. She took a deep breath.

"I am not a spy. In fact, I don't know the Earl of Sutherland. I've never met him—"

"He's nae your guardian?"

"No. I…I'm not from here."

Robbie furrowed his brows. "Are ye from Prussia, then? Or Austria?"

"No, although I have visited those places…" She hesitated. "…just not in this century."

His brows drew closer together. 'I doona understand."

"I don't blame you." Vi took another deep breath. "The reason I know what's going to happen in this war is because I am from the future."

Chapter Fourteen

Robbie hadn't heard correctly. He was sure of it. Or, more likely, she was jesting to avoid the real issue here. "Ye havna answered my question."

"But I have." Vihansa held his gaze. "I am from the future. The twenty-first century, to be exact."

He shook his head. "Ye doona have to invent a story—"

"I'm not. What I say is true."

There was not a trace of amusement in her voice nor in her serious expression. He had the eerie feeling that she meant what she said. "'Tis nae possible."

"Ordinarily, I would agree with you," she replied. "However, since I am here when I haven't been born yet, I have to disagree."

For a moment, he wondered if she was mad, or maybe he'd gone barmy and was having an imaginary conversation with himself. He'd been lusting after Vihansa in the courtyard—thinking how those luscious breasts and rounded bottom would look if he peeled off her clothes—and, since he knew *that* was fantasy, maybe he'd slipped into another realm of delusion.

"You don't believe me."

He blinked rapidly. That was her voice, and unless he had completely lost his mind, she was real, sitting across from him with an earnest look on her face. "How can something like that happen?"

"That's a good question. I don't have an answer." She sighed. "At first, I thought I'd gone through some kind of Time portal when I touched your sword—"

"My sword?" He felt the hilt of the one he was wearing.

"Not that one. The one you were wearing at Hogmanay."

He remembered her odd request that she wanted to see that weapon, shortly after they'd finished the round dance. "Ye think my grandfather's sword held magic?"

"I don't know about magic. It's not something I've believed in, but I do remember brushing my hand across its hilt…and then the world turned hazy and white."

He frowned. "Hazy and white? There was nae fog that night."

"I can't explain. One minute I was on the street, with cars—"

"Cars? Ye mean carts?"

"No. Cars. Automobiles with engines… Never mind that for now." She leaned forward. "What's important is that one minute I was in the twenty-first century, celebrating Hogmanay with my friends, and after the fog or whatever it was went away, I was here." She leaned back. "In the eighteenth century. With you."

Robbie frowned, trying to recall the night himself. There had been a celebration like there was every year. After the procession around the base of the castle, he'd spotted her standing a slight distance away. There had been two friends with her, but they'd gone on ahead. There hadn't been any fog, though. The skies had been clear all night. And there had been no *cars*, whatever they were. Looking at her serious expression, he knew she believed what she'd told him. Yet he had to ask.

"Ye swear this is what you think happened?"

"Think?" She made a sound that sounded like something between a laugh and a cry. "I *know*. I can't explain why I'm sitting here, but I know I am."

He knew she was too. He couldn't deny that she was real. Perhaps he needed to take another tack.

"Why do ye think this happened to ye?"

She brightened. "I'm pretty sure I was sent back to save Scotland."

He gave her a wary look. Perhaps she was truly mad after all. She must have sensed his thinking, because she shook her head.

"That sounded a bit strange, didn't it? I meant... Since the history of Scotland is available in the twenty-first century, I know what is going to happen."

"Ye've read about our Bonnie Prince Charlie, then?"

"Yes, and he's going to be defeated at Culloden unless he can be persuaded to follow Murray's orders." She took a deep breath. "And that's why I think I'm here."

Before he could respond, there was a knock on the door, and he remembered he'd locked it. "Who's there?"

"Anne. Why is the door locked?"

"Just a minute." As he rose, he gave Vihansa a questioning glance. She took another deep breath and nodded. He opened the door.

"Come in, cousin. I think there's something you need to hear."

****

Anne and Vihansa were practicing fencing late in the afternoon several days later when four riders galloped into the courtyard, jubilantly shouting that Fort

Augustus had fallen.

Vi glanced at Anne, who smiled slightly.

"You were right," she said. "I guess we should act surprised."

Vi nodded, knowing this was the proof she needed. She'd already told Anne that the fort would be taken and, to her credit, once Anne had been convinced Robbie was not pulling a prank regarding Vi being from the future, she'd taken the news relatively well. She was still skeptical—not that Vi could blame her since she didn't know herself how she'd gotten here—but Anne had taken a practical approach. She'd asked lots of questions about the prince's future progress and been particularly concerned about Culloden.

"We'll see now if their story matches up with what I said," Vi told her as they walked forward to meet the riders.

"Aye. 'Twill be interesting."

Robbie joined them as the four riders dismounted. He frowned as he looked at her trews, and Vi frowned back. She thought they were over that argument. The pants were so much more comfortable than even the divided riding skirt Anne wore routinely. And she was covered from throat to toe. So, even though the riders were eyeing her, they seemed surprised more than anything. She briefly wondered if she should change, but she wanted to hear their explanation of what happened, to see if history did indeed have it right.

One of the men, who introduced himself as Kyle, sidled up to her as they walked toward the house. "I doona think I've ever seen a lass handle a sword as ye were doing when we rode in."

She smiled. "Lady Mackintosh is a good sparring

partner."

"Aye. I've heard stories about her." He glanced at Anne walking ahead of them, then turned back to Vi. "But how did ye get interested in swordplay?"

She couldn't very well tell him she'd been planning to do a paper on eighteenth-century warfare for her university, so she just shrugged. "My father thought it would be wise for me to learn."

He glanced over her quickly and lifted a corner of his mouth. "And your father approved the trews, as well?"

She wanted to give him a kick in the shins. What was it with men focusing on women in pants? "He did," she said evenly, giving him a challenging look.

He looked like he wanted to reply but perhaps thought better of it, which was wise of him. She really was tired of judgmental males, so she was glad they'd arrived at the entrance to the hall and she was spared further debate on the subject.

Once they were settled in Anne's study with appropriate drinks in everyone's hands, she focused on why they were here.

"It really wasn't much of a battle at all," their leader, a man named Carr, said, "since there were angled bastions at each corner, making the walls weak."

That fit with what Vihansa had read. Cumberland hadn't thought it could be defended—partially because it hadn't been constructed well but also because it sat on a peninsula between the Rivers Oich and Tarff instead of on a hill—which was probably why he was still in Aberdeen. She waited for Carr to go on.

"The prince had three batteries: one firing across the main gate and two from the north," he said. "The prince fired one shot from each for four days, giving the walls time to crumble. Once two of the bastions went down, Major Wentworth surrendered."

That was according to history, too, Vi recalled. Cumberland would consider the major had capitulated too early and have him court-martialed, but that was another story. So far, everything she'd told Robbie and Anne had happened exactly as she had "predicted." She glanced covertly at each of them. Anne looked contemplative and Robbie was frowning. Still, she felt relief that her account had been accurate. Maybe now they'd believe her about the outcome of Culloden.

"Well," Anne said when he'd finished, "I'd like to welcome ye to have dinner and spend the night before ye head back."

"Thank ye," Carr said. "'Twould be good nae to sleep on the ground tonight and get an early start in the morn."

"Good." Anne rose, and so did everyone else. "I'll have Robbie show ye to your quarters, then. Dinner will be in about an hour. We dine simply, in the Great Hall."

As Robbie left with the four men, Anne put her hand on Vi's arm to hold her back. She waited to speak until after the footsteps had faded.

"Everything happened just as ye said it would."

Vi nodded, carefully studying Anne's face. "I'm glad. I know you doubted me."

Anne shook her head. "Nae doubted. 'Tis just…"

"I understand." Vi patted Anne's hand and smiled. "If someone told me she was from the future, I would doubt her sanity. Or maybe my own."

"I did think about that," Anne answered with her own smile.

Vi nodded. "We'll talk more later. Right now, I'd better go and get changed for dinner myself. Robbie will scowl all through the meal if he doesn't see me in a gown."

Anne's eyes twinkled. "I think he'd rather see ye in nothing."

Vihansa felt her face grow warm. She never blushed. But the image Anne created with herself naked with Robbie unexpectedly set her blood on fire.

****

As dinner proceeded, it became obvious to Vi that the guests, with the exception of Carr, were in eighteenth-century terms rather uncouth. They hadn't risen when either she or Anne entered the room, had started eating before everyone was served, and were putting away copious amounts of wine and ale. Their conversation centered on victorious raids and English spoils of war that had been acquired, especially weapons. Not that she minded *that* subject, but it wasn't typical dinner conversation. All in all, though, it had been a fairly entertaining evening, and Cook had liked the fact that her dishes were empty.

The meal had barely concluded when one of the men yawned and stood up. "If ye'll be excusin' me, 'tis been a long day."

Another one rose too. "Aye. I'll be for bed myself since we'll be leavin' at dawn, to ride on."

"Of course," Anne said as the rest of them stood as well. "I'll go talk to Cook about an early breakfast."

Carr glanced at his men, then turned to Robbie and pulled out a flask. "'Tis a bit early for me. Can I interest ye in a dram of whisky? 'Tis pilfered from the fort."

Robbie looked over to Vi, but she waved him on.

She knew he had plenty of questions, but they could wait. She turned to go toward the stairs, but Kyle stepped in front of her.

"Do ye have a minute to spare?" he asked.

She gave him an inquisitive look. "I suppose. Why?"

"I've got a sword with a silver hilt that I took off an English officer. Since I saw ye practice this afternoon, I've been thinking ye should have it."

"I couldn't—"

"Aye, ye could. 'Twould be my pleasure to give it to ye. 'Tis nae every day I see a woman who can wield the weapon like ye did. Besides, 'tis too fancy for me to carry around. 'Twould start brawls." He tilted his head slightly. "At least take a look at it before ye say nae."

"Well, I guess I could do that." Some silver-hilted swords were heirlooms that dated back to the early eighteenth century if not longer. She loved looking at older weapons that were well preserved. "Where is it?"

"I left it with my saddle. 'Twould take just a minute to walk across the yard."

After Robbie's overreaction to finding her in the stall, she wasn't sure she should accompany the man, but she wouldn't be alone with Kyle. Jamie would still be around, making sure the horses had feed and water for the night. Robbie liked to sip his whisky, and she'd be back in just a few minutes anyway.

"All right. Let me get my shawl."

A nearly full moon lit the courtyard as they made their way across it to the stables where a single oil lamp hung carefully suspended from an eave away from anything flammable.

"Jamie?" she called out, since she didn't see him. A

horse nickered and another one stomped a hoof. She turned toward the sounds and noticed the horses were saddled. She frowned. "Jamie should have taken care of your mounts long ago." She called again. "Jamie!"

There was a muffled sound from another of the stalls. As she stepped forward, Kyle suddenly threw an arm around her neck, practically choking her. She clawed at him. "Let…me…go!"

"Aye, I will, but first we'll have a wee bit of fun with ye," he answered.

His words didn't make much sense until she saw the other two men—who'd supposedly gone to bed—emerge from an empty stall.

"Bring her in here," one of them pointed to the stall. "We'll all have a turn with her before we leave."

"And now ye ken why the horses are saddled," Kyle whispered in her ear. "We'll be long gone before anyone finds ye."

Chapter Fifteen

Carr held the flask out. "Do ye care for another?"

Robbie pushed his glass closer to the man. "Doona mind if—" A scream pierced the air, only to be cut off abruptly. In one fluid movement he leapt out of his chair and practically flew through the door as he raced into the courtyard. The sound had come from the stables…

He flung open the door, pausing for a second while his eyes adjusted to the dim light. Then he bellowed like a bull.

Kyle stood in back of Vihansa, his arms under hers and his hands locked behind her neck. She levered herself against him, kicking the man in front of her with both feet, hitting him squarely in his belly. He huffed and started to slump down.

Robbie charged, a fist landing in the man's gut and lifting him up again before tossing him against the wall where he fell and scuttled across the floor and out of the stall like a rat. Robbie swung around just as the second man attacked, and his sideways kick caught the villain in the ribs. The man staggered away, clutching his side and moaning. Robbie straightened and turned to face Kyle, planning to beat the man to a bloody pulp.

The coward held up his hands and backed off. "Nae harm came to her, I swear."

"Which is why I just *might* let ye live." He glanced at Vihansa. Her gown was torn but seemed to be in one piece. "Get out of the way, lass."

Instead, she whirled, one knee going up, connecting strategically with Kyle's manhood, causing him to howl in pain and bend over. Robbie almost started to grin, but stopped. Apparently, Vihansa wasn't quite finished. She bent her arm and, using her weight as ballast, smashed her elbow into Kyle's face. Robbie heard a satisfying crack and saw blood spurting everywhere as the man limped out of range.

Robbie did grin then as he reached out for her and brought her close. "Well done, lass! I couldna have done—"

"What is going on out here?" Carr started to come through the door but jumped back as the three men, who'd managed somehow to get on their horses, galloped out of the stables.

Robbie watched them go, wishing he had enough men to follow them and finish what he'd started. Vihansa was his first priority, though. "Are ye hurt?"

She shook her head as Carr repeated his question.

"What the hell happened?"

Robbie turned to him, trying to read the man. Had he known what his men had been up to? Had he acted as a foil with the offer of whisky? The attack must have been planned, for the three to have been in the stables. It would be a strange coincidence for all of them to have followed Vihansa... He frowned. What had she been doing out in the stables? He shook his head. That answer could wait. Right now, he wanted another answer.

"Your men tried to rape Miss Sutherland." He watched Carr carefully for any telltale sign that he had been aware, but his face blanched and his eyes widened.

"Dear God—"

"Hmmpphh!" The muffled sound came from a stall further down, followed by a thumping sound.

"What the…" Robbie released Vihansa and strode toward the noise. Peering over the bottom half of the door he saw Jamie, arms and legs trussed up and a gag in his mouth, as he tried to roll toward the door. He threw open the door and knelt down beside Jamie, pulling the rag from his mouth as he worked on the knots.

"What happened?"

"I—"

"Farquharson!" Carr called. "I think ye'd best get out here. Your lady just fainted."

****

They were once more assembled in Anne's study—Robbie, Vi, Anne, Jamie, Carr—and Vi felt rather foolish for fainting. Even though it had lasted only a fleeting few seconds, Robbie had carried her into the house and plopped her into Anne's most comfortable chair with a pillow at her back and her feet propped up on a warm brick cushioned on the ottoman. Then he'd put a glass of brandy in her hand. Other than the brandy—which had amazing restorative powers—she felt like a coddled invalid.

Robbie spread a soft tartan across her lap and legs. "Is there anything else ye need?"

"I don't need all this." She took another sip of brandy. "I'm fine."

He frowned. "Ye are nae *fine*. Ye swooned."

"I did not…" Swoon was a word Charlotte would have used in one of her romance novels, but Robbie was being so attentive she didn't want to correct him. "Well, maybe I did, but just for a second or two."

"'Twas enough." He settled in a chair near her and

glared at Carr. "And now, I'm wanting your explanation for this."

"I doona have one." The man swallowed hard, but he didn't look away. "They made a comment or two, but I thought they were jesting."

"What kind of comment?" Anne asked.

The tips of Carr's ears turned pink. "The kind of comments nae fitting for a lady's ears."

Vi took another sip of brandy. "Tell me anyway. I have a right to know why they attacked me."

"I willna use the exact words." He hesitated. "'They thought ye were a loose woman." He paused again. "'Twas because ye were wearing trews."

Vi felt her blood begin to heat, and it had nothing to with the liquor. What gave men the right to judge a woman by what she wore? It was an age-old argument that hadn't been solved in her time either, since blame was still disproportionately attributed to women's apparel "encouraging" advances. She didn't dare look at Robbie, though, because he had tried to warn her.

"'Tis nae her fault for practicing swordplay in comfortable clothing," he said.

She did look at him then. Had he just defended her in spite of telling her numerous times he didn't like her wearing trews? He met her gaze with a slight nod. "'Twas nae your fault, Vihansa."

And he used her name instead of *lass*.

He turned back to Carr. "Ye didna stop them."

"I didna ken what they planned to do. They didna speak of it in front of me."

"And I had nae clue what they intended either." Jamie spoke up for the first time. "Nae until…" His voice trailed off and he looked at Vi. "I'm sorry I couldn't help ye."

"What *did* happen to you?" she asked.

"The three of them came in and said they'd decided nae to wait until morning to spread the news of the victory to the clans further south." He looked sheepish. "I helped them saddle the horses. As I was leading the first one out, I got hit over the head with a musket butt. When I woke up, I was tied and gagged and lying on the floor of the stall." He turned to Vi again. "'Tis sorry I am."

"It wasn't your fault, Jamie. You believed them." Vihansa sighed. "I believed them—or at least, Kyle—too."

Robbie's gaze sharpened. "What did he say to ye?"

"He said since I was interested in weaponry, he wanted to give me a silver-hilted sword that he'd taken from an English officer." Even as she spoke the words, she realized how lame that sounded. "He said he'd left it with his saddle… I thought it would be okay to go to the stables because Jamie would be there." She sighed. "In hindsight, I should have known better."

"Doona blame yourself," Robbie said. "The bloody bastards lured ye there."

For the second time in a matter of minutes, Vi was surprised at Robbie's defense of her. Then she remembered how he had also come to her physical defense in the stall. The sound he'd made would have done a Viking berserker proud, and his charge was nothing short of full battle fury—a Highlander untamed and completely wild in that moment.

"Thank you," she whispered and then turned to Carr. "Your men didn't just try to violate me…they violated the rules of Highland hospitality as well. You do remember Glen Coe, do you not?"

"Aye. The MacDonalds were massacred after offering food and shelter to the English soldiers. But—"

"And once I find them, they'll meet the same fate, in reverse," Robbie growled.

"Good luck with that," Carr replied. "I was going to say those weren't my men. They were mercenaries hired by one of the prince's officers and were on their way back home. That's why they were riding with me."

Robbie narrowed his eyes. "So ye doona ken who they were?"

"Only their first names." Carr shrugged. "And those were probably aliases."

Robbie clenched and unclenched his fists in frustration. Vi recalled the mental image she'd had of him earlier, rushing to her rescue. A wild, untamed highlander. *Her* highlander.

"It's over now." She reached over and laid a hand on his arm. 'Would you help me upstairs? I think I'd like to go to bed."

His expression changed instantly. "Of course. Do ye want me to carry ye?"

"I think I can manage." She smiled inwardly. Tonight, she was going to manage something else as well.

****

Even though Vihansa seemed to have no lingering effects after her ordeal—how he would have loved to pummel each of the mercenaries to within an inch of death—Robbie still kept a hand on her back, one step behind her on the stairs in case she stumbled. Even though she said she could manage on her own, she didn't seem to mind his attentiveness.

He dropped his hand when they got to their room and, as was his custom, waited to disrobe until she was behind the dressing screen. Then he tucked himself into his half of the bed. Usually, he would feign being half-asleep when she emerged in her night rail, but this evening he turned on his side, bolstered on his elbow, and waited. They needed to talk.

It seemed to be taking her longer than usual, or maybe that was because he was staying awake. Then again, maybe she was having trouble undressing because she was hurt and had refused to say so. "Are ye all right?"

There was a rustle behind the screen and then she came around it and he frowned. She was bundled up in the robe she sometimes wore while sitting by the fire reading a book before she went to bed. Had those damn mercenaries scared her so much she didn't feel safe with him in her night shift?

"Ye doona have to be afraid, Vihansa." As much as it pained him to say it, he wanted to reassure her. "I'll nae touch ye. I gave ye my vow."

"Yes, well. About that. I've decided not to hold you to that oath any longer."

She moved toward the bed, undoing the sash at her waist and then letting it slip from her shoulders.

His mouth dropped open. She was naked. Utterly, gloriously, totally naked. "What are ye doing?"

An eyebrow lifted. "I thought it would be rather obvious. Or doesn't seduction work like this in the eighteenth century?"

"Ah…ah…" Words wouldn't come out and he felt like a dolt, but he wasn't sure he was seeing what he thought he was. Maybe he'd been hit in the head earlier and didn't realize it. "Ah…aye." He started to grin.

"Aye, it does."

She smiled and pulled the rolled-up tartan off the bed. "I don't think we'll be needing this any longer either."

Vi crawled across the bed, hoping that Robbie's grin meant he was glad she was doing this. She'd hesitated when she saw his frown as she came around the screen. Maybe she'd misread him all along. Maybe he was content with the situation the way it was. Maybe—she'd almost panicked for a moment—he didn't even find her attractive. Then she'd pushed that thought aside and let the robe fall.

He'd propped himself against the headboard and, as she pulled the blankets down past his waist, she had her answer—if his manhood, already standing at attention, was any indication. She reached over to stroke the length of it, causing him to inhale sharply, which strengthened the chiseled ripples of his abs. Vi smiled, circling the darkened head of his shaft slowly with her thumb, and he growled. She swiped the droplet that appeared and then, looking up at him, licked her finger.

The next thing she knew, she was on her back, her wrists over her head, held there by one of his large hands while the other stroked the side of her before cupping a breast, kneading it while his thumb rubbed the tip. She moaned as the sudden stimulation shot all the way down to her core.

His mouth came down on hers, not exploring or asking permission this time but demanding. Vi felt herself responding by pressing her lips even harder against his until they were both nipping and pulling and sucking, their tongues intertwined in a similar battle. Hungry. Not being able to get enough of each other.

And then he moved to her other breast, his hot mouth covering it, his tongue flicking her nipple as his teeth lightly bit the sensitive skin around it. She arched her back in pleasure, wanting to free her hands so she could run them over his broad shoulders and steel-like biceps, but he held firm. Oddly, the limited ability to move only heightened her senses and she spread her thighs, encircling his hips, and bucked against him.

He raised his head. "I want to take my time with ye."

She shook hers. "Take me. Now." She wiggled her fingers inside his hold. "Like I am."

He studied her for a moment and then she felt him slide inside her. Strong. Bold. Totally filling her. She moaned again, every nerve ending igniting as his thrusts grew deeper and harder. The fire built higher and higher until her entire body felt engulfed in flames. And then, as he suckled once more at her breast, drawing deep, her body shuddered and the volcano within her exploded.

Sparks danced all around her as the tremors slowly subsided. Slowly, she realized he'd released her hands and his weight was no longer on top of her. She opened her eyes to find him lying on his side, watching her.

"That was wonderful." She smiled contentedly. "Much better than I could ever have imagined."

"Aye, 'twas wonderful, but fast, though." He stroked along her ribs, his hand just grazing the side of her breast. "I had thought to pleasure ye more."

"I'm not sure you could pleasure me more."

"Nae?" His mouth quirked up as his thumb brushed across her hardening nipple. "Would ye like for me to show ye I can?"

Her body was already beginning to stir as she reached for him. "*Aye*. Show me."

Chapter Sixteen

Two days later, Vi followed Robbie out into the courtyard where his horse was already saddled and waiting. A message had come that morning from the prince's camp—Prince Charles required his presence. She'd originally thought Robbie "volunteered" to spend time away from Moy Hall to avoid her, but *that* perception had definitely changed over the last two nights. They'd hardly gotten through with the evening meal before each of them came up with an excuse to retire for the evening. Once behind closed—and locked—doors, they'd done everything but retire. Even now, Vi had a pleasant ache between her thighs.

"I'll miss ye, Vihansa," he said they approached his horse and drew her close for a kiss.

A kiss disappointingly short, but there were other people in the courtyard. "I'll miss you too. Hurry back."

"I will." He mounted and leaned down for another quick kiss. "I'll be back as soon as I can."

She watched him ride away, for the first time a little resentful that he was at the prince's beck and call because Anne couldn't attend the council sessions herself.

Now that things had definitely changed between them, she wanted Robbie with her. What the future held—if there was a future—was something she didn't want to think about at the moment. She had planned to allow herself a few days of only pleasurable thoughts…and pastimes. Now she didn't know when he'd be back.

"That interchange was certainly enlightening," Anne said from behind her.

Vi started, feeling her face warm. She hadn't even noticed that Anne had come out, let alone been standing there watching them. She turned with what she hoped was a nonchalant shrug. "Since Robbie defended me so nicely the other night, I decided perhaps a change in attitude was in order."

Anne smiled. "I think there have been some other changes as well."

She felt her cheeks heat again. Good heavens! Had they been heard? Some of their sessions had been rather vocal, and Anne's bedchamber was in the same wing. She tried to muster a degree of dignity. "Previously, I might not have been as pleasant as I should have been, so I thought to make amends."

"That's an interesting way to put it."

Lord, could her face get any hotter without erupting into flame? "I'm…not sure…" She hated when she stammered.

"I'm sorry. I was teasing ye, and I made ye uncomfortable." Anne patted her arm. "Actually, I am glad ye had a change of heart. Robbie's a good man even if he is a bit stubborn. He deserves a good woman."

Vihansa wasn't sure whether to laugh or cry at that, whether it was the revelation that Anne had suspected things weren't great between Robbie and her, or now that things *were*…

Vi took a deep breath. "Was it the kiss you saw that gave it away?"

"Well, that, aye." Anne grinned suddenly. "But the

maid said ye were no longer keeping the bedroll between ye." With that she turned away. "I'll be leaving ye with your thoughts now."

Vi stared after her. The *maid* had known. And by now probably everyone else at Moy Hall did too. And God knew what else they thought of her. She felt a hysterical bubble rise in her throat. She, Vihansa Sutherland—the woman who prided herself on being an independent female beholden to no man—had become one of the moonstruck damsels in Charlotte's novels. What a complete change.

The strange thing was that she wasn't at all sorry about it. The bubble erupted and she started to laugh, right there in the middle of the courtyard.

****

Of all the times to be summoned by the prince, this was not a good one. Robbie was having a hard time concentrating on the discussion taking place among a number of high-ranking officers, regarding a possible attack on Blair Castle. His thoughts kept returning to the past forty-eight hours. To be precise, the *activities* of the past forty-eight hours.

He'd suspected that someone as spirited and independent as Vihansa would be passionate about whatever she did, but he'd hardly expected *quite* such a hellion in bed. Not that he was complaining. Her crawling across the bed naked and then fondling his member before licking that first drop off her fingertip had nearly undone him before they'd even got started. And that was only the beginning.

There was definitely something to be said for having a twenty-first-century bedmate. There was nothing reticent or modest about her participation. She was bold, daring, and—something he found he rather liked—took the initiative as often as he did…and he'd lost track of the number of times. Even now, thinking about their first romp in bed when he returned was making his groin swell.

"And what do ye think?"

The request snapped him out of his reverie and he turned to Iaen MacPherson, chief of the Clan MacPherson, who'd asked the question. He had no idea what had been asked and, considering that Brock and Duff were Iaen's great-uncles and had probably had a sour tale to tell when they returned home, Robbie didn't want to add insult to the clan by not having been listening.

"Is my opinion important?" he ventured. "I'm merely representing Anne."

Iaen gave him a look that left no doubt the man knew he hadn't been attending. Still, to his credit—and maybe because lairds spent a lot of their time settling disputes—he didn't push the subject.

"What do ye think Anne would say, then?" This came from Alex MacGillivray, the man Anne had asked to command the troops she'd mustered. "After all, the Duke of Atholl is General Murray's brother."

Ah. A glimmer of understanding began to take hold. Blair Castle was the seat of Clan Murray, most of whom supported the prince. Unfortunately, James Murray, the present duke, was a government supporter. It made for an awkward situation, at best. And, if the prince was considering attacking the castle, it would pit brother against brother, to say nothing of possibly destroying their home. The prince had commanded both Fort George and Fort Augustus to be burned.

"I think Anne would suggest we ask General Murray how he feels about raiding his family seat."

"General Murray's not here, though," Iaen said. "He's up north, hoping to catch Loudoun before he meets with Cumberland's army."

Robbie held back a sigh. The war was being fought on too many fronts and, if Vihansa was right, the prince was going to find himself in trouble. The Jacobites had marched west and, if rumors had it right, the prince was continuing in that direction to attack Fort William. Right now, he was also thinking about Blair, a bit to the south and had sent Murray north. And they all knew Cumberland was in Aberdeen, to their east.

Robbie shook his head. "I'm nae a tactician, but I would delay a decision until the prince can gather his army and create a master plan to deal with Cumberland, who—in my opinion—is the biggest threat. But I would defer to the generals who are the prince's senior counsel."

"As if the prince would listen," someone at the far end of the table muttered.

Robbie didn't answer. Vihansa had mentioned that would be a problem too.

****

"Oh, my God."

Vi looked up from the book she was reading to see Anne staring into space, still as a statue, a letter crumpled in her hand. She snapped the book closed and hurried over to the desk, realizing she wasn't giving Anne time to answer, but she couldn't stop. "Has something happened to him?"

Robbie had been gone five days, longer than ever before. There had been no word, either, which meant the prince might well have moved his camp or—she'd been avoiding thinking about it—they might have been attacked themselves. Not all Scots supported the Cause, and there were mercenaries out there, as she'd learned all too well.

"Not Robbie." Anne took a deep breath. "Angus. He's been captured."

Vi stared, not quite sure what to say. She knew they were on opposite sides of the war, but Anne didn't speak often about her husband. The few times she had, it had been with kindness and no animosity. "Is he…all right?" she finally managed.

"I…think so." Anne smoothed out the letter. "He apparently had joined Loudoun. Approximately three hundred men were taken. Angus's regiment was a part of them."

Vi knew that regiment was one of three known as the Black Watch, groups of Highlanders basically hired by the Crown to keep other Highlanders in check. Depending on which Scots held them, it wasn't an enviable spot to be in. "Does it say where he is?"

'Somewhere in Sutherland."

How ironic, Vi thought, considering her last name. She felt a twinge of guilt even though her direct family was in the twenty-first century. "Do you think they'll be taken to Dunrobin Castle since there are so many of them?"

"I doona ken." Anne crumpled the letter again. "I guess time will tell us."

****

It had been a very long week. Robbie had been just about ready to head back to Moy Hall when the news came that the Black Watch regiment had been captured, along with English soldiers. While that victory kept several hundred men from joining in Cumberland's ever-growing forces, it was a quandary as to what to do with them. Most of them were Scottish, even if they served the government. Clan blood was strong, whether members were on opposing sides or not. Still, they couldn't just be allowed to go free. There had been heated arguments among the commanders about the issue, with no final decision reached other than that they would temporarily be housed at Dunrobin. All except one.

Robbie looked over to Angus Mackintosh, riding beside him. The prince had decided—out of respect to Anne—that he would release her husband into her custody.

It would be quite the homecoming.

****

Vi and Anne both grounded their swords in the courtyard as they heard horses approach. Robbie! She tried not to show her excitement, especially since Anne had been in a somber mood since they'd received the letter several days ago. This was actually the first day Vi had been able to convince her that a fencing workout was just the thing she needed. Robbie was back, but for Anne's sake, she would be the model of decorum until they were alone. She squinted as the horses entered the courtyard. "Who is that with Robbie?"

Anne didn't answer. When Vi looked at her she was in statue mode again. "Anne? What is it? Do you know who that is?"

Her words seemed to break the spell. Anne smiled. "Aye. I do." Then she walked forward to wait for the horses.

The man who dismounted had a touch of silver to his hair, but his stance was that of a soldier. He walked over to Anne and bowed.

Anne dipped her head. "Your servant, Captain."

"Nae," he answered. "Your servant, Colonel."

She smiled slightly. "Perhaps we should go inside."

"Perhaps we should."

As Anne turned and led the way, Vi looked at Robbie. "Who is that?"

He grinned. "That would be Anne's husband."

Vi felt her mouth drop open and she snapped it shut. Talk about her own decorum and closed doors. She wondered what would be going on behind Anne's tonight.

Chapter Seventeen

Vi had been hoping that, with Angus' return, she might be able to get some information regarding Cumberland's plans, but his only reply had been that he hadn't been in Aberdeen and was not privy to those.

Not that she'd seen much of him. He kept himself pretty much secluded in the suite of rooms he shared with Anne, and she'd been close-lipped too, other than to say her husband was doing a lot of reflection. Vi hadn't questioned her further.

She hadn't seen much of Robbie either, since the prince had appointed him a special civilian counselor to their marathon strategy-planning sessions, presumably to take the prince's side when he didn't agree with his military officers. Robbie'd just gotten home this morning. God knew when he'd have to leave again.

She looked up now as he entered the solar where she'd been enjoying the warmth of the late afternoon sun as it streamed through a window. Outside, the world lay blanketed in snow from a late spring blizzard that had howled through overnight.

"Did the prince decide to march on to Fort William after all?"

"Aye." Robbie sank into the chair opposite hers, looking tired. "I tried to persuade him it would be better to keep the troops at Inverness and prepare for Cumberland's eventual move, but he wouldna have it."

"Not surprising, I guess." Vi sighed. "I'm worried, though, that he will not listen to advice when he should."

Robbie looked at her. "Tell me again what the history books say."

She took a deep breath. "Culloden will be a disaster, due to confusion among the ranking officers giving orders. The Highland Charge is not organized and the British run the men down with their cavalry. The whole thing will be over in less than an hour." She closed her eyes, then opened them again. "Fifteen hundred Scots will die."

There was silence following her statement.

"Am I one of them?" Robbie finally asked.

"I don't know." She got up and went over to him, crawling into his lap when he opened his arms. "I don't want you to go. Promise me you won't."

He stroked a stray hair away from her face. "I canna make that promise."

"Why not? You aren't in the army."

"That doesna matter anymore." He brushed a kiss across her forehead. "The prince depends on me now."

"Then he should listen to you." She frowned. "The battle at Culloden—on Drummossie Moor—cannot happen."

"I'll keep trying to convince him." He pulled her closer and nuzzled her throat. "But I canna do it now."

"No, but—"

"Vihansa. Can ye think of nothing better to do at the moment than fash?"

"Umm…ooh," she said as he nibbled the corner of her mouth and sensation shot through her. She curled her hand around his neck. "I think I can."

****

Once more, Robbie found himself away from home, this time on the Ardgour peninsula near the Corran Narrows in Loch Linnhe, about nine miles from Fort William. The intent was to block any transport of English munitions or supplies to the fort.

He looked around the group of men—General Murray and Colonel Stapleton, with Donald Cameron and Alexander MacDonald, the lairds of Lochiel and Keppoch, respectively—gathered with himself and Prince Charles in one of the tents that had been erected. They'd been debating—he should just use the word *arguing*, except the prince was not allowing anyone to actually shout or yell this morning.

"I doona think this fort can be taken," Stapleton said.

"Do ye plan to let the English keep on raiding our lands, then?" one of the lairds asked.

"They've already destroyed property and taken livestock," the other one said.

"I understand your concern." The colonel sighed. "The other forts had weaknesses in design. The foundation at Fort George was unstable and the angle of the bastions at Fort Augustus was more for show than defense. We willna have the same luck taking this one. Fort William is too well fortified."

"Aye, I agree," Murray said.

If the situation hadn't been so heated, Robbie would have grinned. It wasn't often that the general and the colonel agreed. Even the prince looked somewhat surprised.

The lairds both turned to Charles. "We've supported ye, both with men and equipment. We need your help now to maintain our lands."

The prince looked uncomfortable and Robbie felt a

159

twinge of sympathy. The lairds could not be blamed for making their request. Preservation of land was everything for a clan. Highlanders also had a strong sense of honor and expected support from those they'd supported. On the other hand—and Vihansa had made the point clear—Charles needed to be concentrating on the eastern half of Scotland right now. Cumberland was posing a bigger threat every time he amassed more troops.

His thoughts drifted to her. Their lovemaking had taken on an intensity he'd never known before. Not only was Vihansa completely uninhibited—and she made some suggestions he hadn't even thought about doing—but she was totally passionate, hardly waiting for both of them to recover before she would stroke him again. Sometimes he felt her need almost as desperation…that she wanted to prolong each episode as long as she could for fear there wouldn't be another.

That thought sobered him. According to her, well over a thousand Scots would die on the battlefield at Culloden if nothing were done to alter history. He looked at the prince again. The man was young and he'd never seen battle before coming to Scotland. He hadn't even grown up in Scotland, having only arrived on her shores less than a year ago. Robbie certainly couldn't see him leading a Highland Charge, but would he trust the wisdom and experience of his commanders and allow them to make the decisions? According to Vihansa, it was critical that he did. Lives depended on those decisions, to say nothing about the fate of Scotland itself.

"Do you have an opinion?

Robbie realized the prince was talking to him. He shifted uncomfortably in his seat. Sometimes he really wished the prince hadn't appointed him a civilian counselor, but then, it was precisely because of situations like this that Charles *had* appointed him. To be the arbitrator between the military and the clans.

"I suggest we continue with the blockade for now. A type of siege from a distance. If we can stop what arrives at Fort William, we may be able to force a surrender. At the least, the English will be trying to get around the blockade, which will keep them busy."

Neither of the lairds looked very happy and neither did the general and colonel, but the prince smiled. "Hear, hear! I think it's an excellent idea."

From the look of disgruntlement on every other face, none of them agreed, but—for now—it seemed they were willing to hold their collective peace.

He sighed inwardly. All he wanted to do was go home to Vihansa.

****

When Robbie rode in the next afternoon, he looked tired. Vi had hoped she could whisk him upstairs where she'd ordered a hot bath to be waiting for him…one that she would join him in and make sure he'd feel much better when they were through. She'd spent the better part of the last several days thinking about a sexy watery scenario.

Unfortunately, Anne asked him to come to the study immediately. Vi assumed she was anxious to hear how things had progressed. Now that Angus was home—and out of danger—Anne had become increasingly more interested in the prince's strategy. Once they were all seated, she glanced at Vi before turning to Robbie.

"Is Fort William still standing?"

Vi had already told her that Fort William would not

be destroyed like the other two had been, but if she were in Anne's shoes, she'd be skeptical about information from the "future" too.

"Aye. They've blockaded the Narrows so the English ships canna deliver goods to the fort."

"A siege of sorts, then," Anne said. "How long do they intend to stay there?"

"I doona ken." He glanced at Vi. "The general and colonel were a bit at loggerheads with the lairds on what to do."

She gave him a subtle nod of understanding. *That* was what was the root of the whole Jacobite problem. Usually, it was the military officers who didn't agree with each other, but the clans were fiercely independent too, and wary of allowing the army, albeit a Scottish one, to control them. It didn't help that the prince they were fighting for was practically a foreigner, even if he was a Stuart. They'd discussed this before he'd left.

"Is there any chance they'll be returning soon, do ye think?" Anne asked.

"'Tis hard to say," he replied. "Why? Have ye news about Cumberland?"

"Nae. But…" She reached into a drawer and pulled out a paper. "I received this just this morning."

Vi frowned. They hadn't had any visitors that she was aware of, but then, there was a shadow network of sorts that operated much like when Lachlan had brought the news that Loudoun was on his way to Moy Hall.

Robbie leaned forward. "What does it say?"

Anne handed him the missive. "The English captured the French ship *Embascade*." She sighed. "I know the prince was counting on more French support."

"Aye." Robbie sighed too. "He mentioned he'd

asked King Louis for reinforcements."

Which probably wouldn't be coming. Once King Louis heard his ship had been taken, it would be surprising if he sent another. It was something she'd have to discuss with Robbie later. *Later* being the key word. She stood.

"If you'll excuse us, Anne, I'd like a private word with Robbie."

A mischievous twinkle flickered in Anne's eyes as Robbie rose too. "I suspect it might be more than words ye want to have in private."

Vi gave her a wide smile, not embarrassed in the least. "You may be right."

Robbie grinned as he followed her out. "What do ye have in mind?"

"You'll see," she said. The bath water might be only lukewarm by now, but she planned on having it steaming in no time.

****

When a messenger arrived two weeks later, Vi wasn't surprised by the news that the prince had decided to retreat. The history books were becoming frighteningly accurate. Still, she sat quietly listening to the man give his account to Anne and Robbie.

"We started firing on the fort a couple of days after we blockaded the Narrows," he said, "but with the poor road conditions, we couldna bring in the heavy cannon."

"With as thick as those walls are, that couldna have been very effective," Robbie said.

"Aye. 'Twasn't," the messenger answered, "but we thought we might be putting some fear into them when the commander was replaced ten days later by a captain of Guise's regiment."

Vi considered that. Guise's regiment was an old, established one known for well-trained infantry which, in the case of a siege, was a lot more important than having cavalry. However, they were stationed in the northeast of Scotland and Cumberland hadn't sent them as reinforcements. He'd sent them—along with the captain—as replacement for the current officer in charge. The messenger could be right. The duke might have felt pressure to make sure the last fort remained standing. Or—more likely—he saw the siege as an annoyance and something that needed a quick squashing.

"How did that turn out?" Anne asked

"We managed to move our smaller cannons to Sugarloaf and Cow Hill, closer to the fort, and got some good rounds off. Scott sent more than a hundred of his men out to counterattack, but we were prepared for that." He grinned. "The Sassenach retreated behind the fort's walls."

Vi looked at the messenger, pretty sure she knew the answer to the question she was going to ask. "If the Jacobites were holding their own, why did the prince not choose to stay the course?"

The man's grin faded. "General Murray received word that Cumberland had begun his march west and ordered the army back to Inverness."

Vi exchanged a look with Robbie who nodded imperceptibly. They'd previously discussed if the prince could be convinced to hold fast at Inverness and make Cumberland come to him, there was a chance the Scots would be victorious and Culloden would never happen. That hopeful theory hinged on whether or not the prince could be persuaded.

Today's date was April 3. Time was running out.

Chapter Eighteen

"Do you think you've made any kind of headway?" Vi asked Robbie a week later after he'd returned from a meeting with the prince and his command staff.

"I doona ken." Robbie hated the look of dismay he saw on Vi's face and pulled her closer to him on the divan in the parlor. "He didna outright say nae to the idea."

She nestled against his shoulder. "But he didn't say yes."

"I think the prince is confused and doesna ken what to do."

Vi lifted her head. "That's not exactly a sterling quality in a man who wants to claim the crown. What do his commanders say?"

"Och, they argue as always," Robbie replied. "One wants to engage in trench warfare like Robert the Bruce did—"

"There is an advantage to attacking in small bands and vanishing before the enemy can respond," Vi said, "especially when the English government is larger and better equipped."

"Aye, but the prince is nae happy with that idea."

Vi sighed. "What are the other options they're considering, then?"

"The general thinks the army should assume a defensive position by the ravine at Dalcross Castle, and one of the colonels prefers an open field for combat." He heard Vihansa's sharp inhale.

"Not Culloden," she whispered.

He hesitated, then nodded. "The suggestion was Drummossie Moor just next to Culloden House."

"But it's boggy. How in the world would those officers think a Highland Charge would be effective?"

"Their argument was that it would be worse for the English cavalry to charge."

"But it won't." Vi gave him a desperate look. "You somehow have to convince the prince of that. Make him choose somewhere else—*anywhere* else." Her voice trembled. "Then we may have a chance."

Robbie wrapped both arms around her and tucked her head beneath his chin. "I'll keep trying. Ye have my oath."

****

From the look on Robbie's face when he returned from his last meeting with the prince and his commanders, Vi doubted he'd been successful, but she stayed quiet until they were all seated in Anne's study.

"You might as well give us the bad news first."

"Which piece of bad news do ye want first?"

Vi stared at him, her stomach sinking to her feet. "Which piece? I'm not sure I want to know, but what went wrong?"

Anne raised a hand to wait, then got up and went over to the decanter of whisky standing on a nearby shelf. She poured a dram each for herself and Vi and poured two for Robbie. "It sounds like you might need this," she said as she handed him his glass and returned to the desk, where she took a healthy sip of her own.

He downed his in one swallow, then closed his eyes

to either savor the moment or give himself a chance to regain his breath. Then he shook his head.

"The prince and his commanders are still arguing about which strategy to use, Cumberland is on the march here, and Cromartie's men have been captured." He looked from Vi to Anne. "Which story do ye want first?"

"We know about the first two," she answered. "What happened to Cromartie? I thought he was still occupying Dunrobin."

"He was, but he'd gotten word that Cumberland was on the move, so with Sutherland no longer a threat—or so he thought—he decided to bring his several hundred men to Inverness to join the prince. They were ambushed on the way."

"By whom?" Vi asked.

"Evidently nae all of Sutherland's men fled when he did after Cromartie laid claim to Dunrobin. They were hiding in the hills all this time."

Vi frowned. "But there couldn't have been hundreds of them to attack his men."

"According to the soldier that got through to Inverness, they numbered about half of Cromartie's men."

"Then why weren't they defeated?"

Robbie sighed. "It seems that the commanding officers were a bit lax. Since they'd not perceived a threat about Sutherlands hiding in the hills, they'd allowed the foot soldiers to march on ahead. Having horses, they felt they could catch up at any time."

Anne downed the rest of her drink. "Let me guess. The officers got separated from their men and left a convenient opening for an ambush."

"Aye. The spot they chose was a pass between the

hills at Golspie by Littleferry. It didn't take many of them to cut the officers off from their troops."

"And without orders, the men didn't fight." Anne said this more as a statement than a question.

"Their orders were to go to Inverness."

"That's what they did?" Vi asked.

Robbie shook his head. "Some of them stayed to fight, or tried to, but with no senior officers to direct them, it was chaos."

Just like Culloden will be. Vi closed her eyes. Prince Charlie wouldn't give the command to charge and the front line would take matters into their own hands, separating into three groups with the center charging forward. Unfortunately, the right flank would be cut off by a walled enclosure and forced toward the left, which put them directly in front of the charge. Chaos would ensue and the English cavalry would take advantage of it. The battle would be over almost before it began, but hundreds of men would die and Scotland would never be independent again. Vi took a deep breath and opened her eyes.

"If the history books are accurate, we have just two days to prevent a massacre at Culloden." She drew another shaky breath. "Just two days."

****

"The prince cannot do that."

Vi's remark was met with silence in the Jacobite headquarters as several pairs of eyes turned on her. Some were skeptical, some raised brows questioningly, and others narrowed theirs. Only Robbie's expression remained stoically neutral.

Not that she was surprised at any of their reactions. Robbie had not wanted her to come to Inverness to plead the case against Drummossie Moor for a battleground. It was the only argument they'd had since they'd started sharing intimacy. He'd said that, at best, the generals and colonels and even lairds would laugh her out of the room. At worst, they'd squelch her ideas in harsh terms, if they actually allowed her to talk. He'd pointed out, once again, that even Anne, who held the military rank of colonel, wasn't allowed to sit at counsel. Vi had replied hotly that it was about time the commanders did listen to a female and any insults they might hurl would sail right past her.

And they had allowed her to speak. Whether they were nonplused that she had the audacity to appear or whether they thought having a woman spouting military strategy might be entertaining, she didn't know nor did she care. She had said what she'd come to say.

"The prince must not fight Cumberland on that moor," she said again.

"I agree with ye," one of the generals finally said.

"And I doona," a colonel said.

Vi looked at him in frustration. "Why? Do you really think you have an advantage on a wide open space?"

"Aye. 'Tis what's needed for a Highland Charge."

"But the prince won't—"

"Perhaps the idea needs to be presented to him once more," Robbie cut in.

Vi bit her lip. She'd almost said that the prince would not order the charge and *that* revelation would have been pure disaster in more ways than one. She'd hardly been able to conceal her disappointment that the prince was not here, but she'd been told he was in conference with a courier who'd arrived from the western port city where the French ships should have arrived. It was already too late for that, not that King Louis was sending any more ships. She sighed and turned to the general.

"Since you agree with me, perhaps you could talk to the prince?"

He nodded. "I will try. We know Cumberland arrived in Nairn yesterday. We still have time to stake out a more strategic location—one more to our advantage—to await him." He looked at the others and then back to her. "If ye'll excuse us, there are some other matters we need to discuss."

"Of course." She rose, knowing she was being dismissed and hoping he wouldn't dismiss her idea once she'd left.

Robbie escorted her out to the carriage that awaited. He helped her inside, then stepped back. "Doona fash. I'm going to stay and find out what plans are actually made."

"Thank you! Thank you!" She leaned out the door and captured his face for a kiss, not caring that the footman and driver were watching. "Thank you!"

His hands cradled her head as he prolonged the kiss, oblivious to the chuckles from the two men. Then slowly he pulled back and shut the door. "Until later, then."

She nodded. "Until later."

Restless for most of the afternoon, Vi grew more worried as each hour passed. By the time dinner was on the table, she was too nervous to eat.

"Why do you think Robbie hasn't returned?" she asked Anne again after far too many other times.

"I suspect they're making last-minute decisions."

"More likely, last-minute arguments," Vi said.

"There is nothing we can do now except pray the prince listens to reason." She looked at her husband who, as usual, did not take part in their conversations. "How soon do you think Cumberland will make his move?"

Angus shook his head. "I canna say, but probably it willna be today since it's the duke's birthday. He'll nae doubt be celebrating it."

In Nairn. Suddenly, Vi's blood chilled as she remembered an important fact in this battle. She knew now why Robbie hadn't come home. The general must not have been successful in convincing the prince, and he would soon be making the first mistake that would lead to Scotland's defeat. How could she have forgotten that the Jacobites, taking advantage of Cumberland celebrating his birthday, would attempt a twelve-mile march to Nairn to surprise him before dawn?

Lord. Had her interference made this happen? Like the time-traveler in Ray Bradbury's story about a man who'd stepped off the path and crushed a butterfly, thereby changing the outcome of history? She felt almost nauseous as she realized she might even have encouraged that decision inadvertently by dissuading him from using the moor for a battlefield. Robbie would be marching with them.

And so would she. Once Anne and Angus had gone to bed, she'd leave. She could probably catch up to them if she rode. She had to at least try.

It would be her last chance to avert the certain fate that awaited.

****

This had to be one of the worst hare-brained ideas that had come up during this war. Robbie looked around at the men who were marching toward Nairn. They were bedraggled, tired, and hungry since, after the morning talks broke down, the prince had decided the army would march to Drummossie Moor and *wait* for Cumberland to appear. They'd have the element of surprise, he'd said. When the general hadn't shown up by dusk, Robbie assumed common sense would take over and they'd return to camp, get a good night's sleep, and be prepared to fight in the morning, even though the moor was still a poor choice.

But no. The prince seemed fixated on having the element of surprise and had ordered the weary men to march to Nairn in the night and attack Cumberland before dawn. Robbie had hoped that if he went along he'd be able to dissuade the prince within a mile or two, especially since the temperature was dropping fast and it had started sleeting, adding to the misery. Instead, he'd been ordered to the rear ranks to make sure no one deserted during the march. He had half a mind to do just that himself.

Then he remembered Vihansa. Leaving the men to march on without at least trying one last time to intervene was not an option. He would just have to keep the thoughts of her—their naked bodies intertwined beneath heavy blankets in front of a roaring fire—to keep him warm on this frigid night. Right now, though, he needed to try and get to the prince.

"Did ye hear that?"

Robbie looked at the soldier beside him who'd asked.

"Hear what?"

"Someone's coming up behind us."

He cocked his head to one side. Faintly, he heard something that could be hoofbeats. "Aye. A rider?"

The other man stopped walking and pulled his musket.

Robbie glanced at it. "Why are ye doing that? 'Tis likely one of the prince's men with a message." He hoped it was serious enough to cause the prince to retreat.

The soldier gave him a look that said he clearly didn't understand war. "'Tis more likely to be a redcoat returning to Nairn from surveillance."

Robbie had to admit that made more sense. "Well, he'll find the road blocked, won't he?"

The man shook his head. "If he sees us, he'll ride around, and one horseman can get to Nairn faster than we can. Cumberland will be warned."

That probably made sense too. "What do ye plan to do?"

"Hide. Wait. Ambush." The man stepped off the road toward some trees. Robbie gave a quick look to the men up ahead who were disappearing around one of the many bends in the road, and then he followed the soldier since he was under orders not to allow anyone to leave. The sound of a horse galloping was becoming louder. "Let's make sure it is a redcoat before ye shoot."

The man gave him a look that said he clearly must be daft. "With as cold as it is, a man—especially a weakly Englishman—will be wearing a heavy coat. Ye willna be seeing much red. Ye ken?"

"Aye, but ye still need to make sure."

This time the soldier didn't answer him at all. He simply raised his musket, leveling it as the rider came closer.

Snow was now mixing with the sleet and the wind had picked up. The swirling mess made it hard to see very far ahead in the dark. Robbie brushed the wetness away from his eyes and squinted.

A horse and rider thundered around the last curve they'd just passed. He could barely make out a hooded figure with a cloak streaming behind. Somehow, the figure looked familiar…

A shot rang out, nearly deafening him. Then a woman screamed. *Vihansa*!

The soldier looked stunned for a moment and then he took off running. Even though Robbie ached to throttle the man, it would have to wait. Vihansa had been hurt. He hurried over to where she lay in a heap on the ground, not moving.

"Vihansa! *Mo cridhe*, please doona be dead!" He knelt and turned her over gently, then stifled a gasp at the amount of blood already soaking through her cloak. He pressed his hand against her shoulder to try and stop the flow and her eyes fluttered open.

"Robbie…" she whispered.

"Hush, *cuisle m' fhuil*, doona talk. Save your breath."

"I'm…too…late…" she murmured, her eyes closing as she went still.

"Nae!" He bent down to kiss her cold lips. "Nae! *Mo anam cara!*"

"Aye. She is your soulmate," a female voice said, "and she is also the pulse of your heart as ye said."

For a moment, Robbie was sure he had gone barmy and was hearing things. Slowly, he looked up. And blinked. He *had* gone barmy in his grief, for the woman standing in front of him was the auburn-haired lady he'd seen briefly at the ceilidh.

"What…Bridgid?" He shook his head. What was the

woman from the ceilidh doing on a battlefield? "Why are ye here?"

She smiled. "I heard your call."

"My call?" He clutched Vihansa's lifeless body to him. "Unless ye can bring my love back to me, I doona care."

"I can do that."

He blinked again. She sounded quite calm and rational. Clearly, grief had overtaken him and he was not right in his head. He was hearing—and probably seeing—something that wasn't happening. Or maybe…maybe it was Vihansa's ghost?

"Are ye my love's ghost?"

She shook her head. "Your Vihansa yet lives, in another time."

He stared at her, sure his sanity was rapidly leaving him. "Ye ken she's from the future?"

"Aye. I brought her here. I can send her back." Bridgid tilted her head. "The question is do ye want to go with her? To her time?"

If he had taken leave of his senses, he wasn't going to fight it anymore. Better to live in a new reality where Vihansa was still alive. "Send both of us."

"Ye are sure?"

"I doona want to live in this life without Vihansa."

Bridgid nodded and lifted both hands to the heavens. *"Gum Faigh Thu Sith, Taibhse a Culloden."*

The snow and sleet gathered into a whirlwind enveloping them as they disappeared into the mist.

The goddess smiled once more. "May ye find peace, Ghost of Culloden."

Epilogue

Vi snuggled closer to Robbie, burrowing her head against him as she turned on her side to lay a hand on his chest.

"Ouch!" Her eyes flew open as a sharp pain flashed through her shoulder.

"Careful, *mo cridhe*." Robbie gently shifted her. "Ye've been shot."

"What?" She tried to sit up, but his arms were holding her and she fell back. Then, as her gaze began to focus on the ceiling above her, she felt the room tilt. Closing her eyes until the sensation went away, she slowly opened them again and looked around.

She was home. In her bedroom. In the twenty-first century. And Robbie was *here*. With her. In *her* century. She felt her eyes widen as she looked at him.

"You aren't a ghost, are you?"

He smiled. "Only if ye are."

She took in the sight of him, still dressed in Highland gear. His muddy boots stood next to her chair, his sword and targe propped up against the dresser. Then she glanced down at what she was wearing, shocked to see the brown stains of dried blood on the wool gown she still wore. The one she'd worn while riding to Nairn...

"What happened?"

He leaned over to kiss the tip of her nose, then wrapped his arms tighter around her. "Ye were shot by an eejit who thought ye were the enemy. I told him to hold his fire until we could see ye, but he didna listen. The coward fled afterward. I'd have killed him but I needed to tend to ye."

"I'm glad you didn't." Vi looked down at her gown again. "Am I badly injured?"

"Nae anymore, but…" Robbie hesitated.

"But what?"

"What do ye remember?"

She frowned. She'd been riding hard to catch up to the army. "I remember seeing torches up ahead and then they disappeared around a bend. I remember rounding the curve and then there was a flash of bright light. I felt a searing pain… Then you were holding me…and then, a calming stillness settled over me." Her frown deepened. "Was that when I was shot?"

"Aye." He took a deep breath. "Ye died, Vihansa."

A shock went through her. She remembered nothing after that feeling that all was well. That there was nothing to worry about any longer.

"Are we both dead, then?" She waved her good arm. "Is none of this real? Am I only thinking I'm having this conversation in the twenty-first century?"

"Doona fash. Ye—we—are nae dead." He stroked her hair, tucking an unruly curl behind her ear. "And this…" He indicated her room. "Is real. And aye, we are in your time."

"But how…" She looked around again, spying the sword. It was the same sword Robbie had been wearing at Hogmanay, the one she'd touched. "Was it the sword that brought us back?"

He furrowed his brows, then shook his head. "Nae. The sword had nothing to do with it. 'Twas Bridgid."

"Bridgid?"

"Aye. Ye remember the lass who led the precession around the castle at Hogmanay?"

"You mean the one with the long auburn hair?"

"Aye—"

"Wait!" Sudden recognition struck her. "Wasn't she the one who was also at the first ceilidh, and we thought she was part of the prince's entourage?"

"Aye," he said again, "only she wasn't with the prince."

Vi definitely remembered her talking to Robbie. "Why is she important?"

"She's the one who brought ye to me," Robbie replied, "and she's the one who sent us back."

"But how…" Vi stopped. If she thought a sword had the magical qualities of Excalibur, she supposed it wasn't that far a stretch to think a person might. She *had* traveled through Time. Apparently twice. "Who is she?"

"I believe she is the ancient Celtic goddess Bridgid."

The woman Vi remembered certainly wasn't *ancient,* but perhaps this wasn't a time for semantics. She did recall from history that both the Celts and the Norsemen who settled in northern Scotland had worshipped her. She was a fertility goddess known as the Wise Woman who could divine the future. When Christianity had taken hold, she was transformed into Saint Bridget.

Vi wrinkled her brow. "But how is she involved?"

"I was holding ye…sure that ye were dead. I was grieving that I had lost ye, *mo anam cara.*" He was quiet a moment. "And then *she* was there. Bridgid said she could send ye back…that ye would live in your time. And then she asked if I wanted to go with ye."

Vi arched a brow at him. "I take it you said yes?"

"I did." He ran his fingers lightly across her cheek. "I want to be with ye in my time or yours. It doesna matter which, as long as we are together."

"I agree." Vi snuggled closer against him, then lifted her head. "Wait. What did you just call me? Mo something?"

"*Mo anam cara*. It means ye are my soulmate."

"Mmmm. I like the idea of that." And, to her own surprise, she truly did. This was a man she wanted to spend eternity with, regardless of what century they were in.

****

Vi gave Robbie a covert look as they took a table near the back of a popular coffee shop to wait for Charlotte to arrive. She'd had a voice mail on her phone after she "got back" saying Charlotte wanted to meet her because she had some unbelievable news. Vi didn't think it would be any more unbelievable than what had happened to her, but she'd let Charlotte go first. After all, you didn't just announce you'd travelled back in Time. Or that you'd brought a sexy Highlander home with you.

Luckily, since her house was located off a gravel road on part of a small ranch her parents had once owned, Robbie's first day in the future had been a fairly easy adjustment. Her home—once the foreman's cottage—was an isolated place with horses and cattle grazing nearby, and the Texas wheat fields were similar to Scottish barley. He had remarked that it wasn't much different from Scotland, except for the lack of mountains.

That had changed when she'd shown him her SUV. He'd been adamant that he wasn't about to get into a metal box on wheels. It had taken a couple of days of coaxing—and a night of steamy sex in the folded down rear of the vehicle—to convince him that the "machine" had its advantages.

She hadn't told him about the traffic they'd encounter enroute to the coffee shop. From the expression on his face—and the fact that he'd gone pale—she suspected she'd be getting quite an earful about that later.

"I can't wait for you to meet Charlotte," she said now as a way to distract him. "She's one of my best friends."

"Hmph."

It wasn't much of an answer, but it was better than the total silence she'd been enduring. "Charlotte is a romance writer. Isn't that interesting?"

"Hmph."

She tried again. "My other best friend is Athena, but it seems she's out of town. Charlotte couldn't get hold of her."

"Hmph."

Vi sighed. She couldn't really blame him for being a bit surly. She should have warned him about traffic, but she didn't think he'd actually have gotten in the car if she had. Still, the sight of all those trucks and cars whizzing by at seventy miles an hour must have scared him, not that he'd admit it. She just hoped that, when Charlotte appeared, Robbie would contribute a little more to the conversation.

As if her thought had conjured her, she saw Charlotte coming through the door. "Oh, good! She's here!" She turned to Robbie, about to ask him to be nice—they could settle their little dispute later—but he was staring at her friend with nothing short of amazement. She frowned. Her friend was very pretty, but…

"Fraser?" Robbie stood up, nearly toppling the chair.

Vi looked back to Charlotte and noticed a man—a very handsome one—standing behind her. He looked dumbfounded too.

"Farquharson?" The man advanced, holding out his hand. "Is it really ye?"

Another Highlander? He spoke with a definite burr. It was Vi's turn to be confounded. She looked at Charlotte, who was now staring at Robbie.

Understanding began to sink in. "Charlotte, have you been…*away*?"

Her friend turned to her. "You wouldn't believe how far away I've been."

"Hmmm. I think I might." Vi gestured to the two men who were now conversing fast, but quietly. "Is that hunk with you from the eighteenth century?"

Charlotte's eyes widened. "Yes. How did you know…" She stopped, a smile beginning to form on her face as she took in Robbie's appearance and looked back at Vi. "Is your hottie from there too?"

Vi nodded. "It seems we might have the same story to tell."

Charlotte sank down into an empty chair. "I didn't think any of this was possible, but somehow, during that Hogmanay dance—"

"The one led by Bridgid the goddess?"

Charlotte's eyes widened again. "So she took you back too?"

"Yes." Vi glanced at the men again, still standing

and whispering frantically. "It seems that our Highlanders know each other."

"It makes sense, I guess, since both clans fought for Bonnie Prince Charlie." Charlotte's expression grew sad. "I hoped I could change the outcome of history, but Niall was wounded in battle at Culloden and we were sent back."

"I thought that's why I'd been sent back, too. Preventing the battle on Drummossie Moor would have made all the difference." Vi grew somber. "I was shot the day before. Robbie says I actually died before Bridgid sent us home."

Charlotte chewed her lip. "I suppose Athena might still have a chance."

"Athena? Do you think she's in the eighteenth century too?"

"It makes sense. Why would only two of us go back in Time?"

Vi considered. It did make sense. The three of them had been together that night. Each of them had met a rugged Highlander. Why wouldn't Athena have gone through the mist with hers? "Well, then, I guess we'll wait for Athena."

"It'll be interesting to see if Athena returns with *her* Highlander in tow." Charlotte tapped her lips with a finger and then began to grin. "I feel a good romance novel coming out of all this. Hunky, sexy Highlanders…" Her voice trailed off as her eyes took on a faraway look that meant she was already plotting.

Vi laughed. "Write your romance, then."

Meanwhile, she planned on putting real romance back into her life as soon as she got Robbie home. He wouldn't be silent for long, once she did.

Afterword

Anne Mackintosh's appointed captain, Alexander Macgillivray, was killed at the Battle of Culloden, as were a number of the troops she'd recruited. A marker stands today on the battlefield near the Well of the Dead.

The only female officer in the Jacobite army, Anne was arrested after the defeat at Culloden and, ironically, turned over to the custody of her husband. Their marriage seemed to be an amicable one, in spite of being on opposing sides of the war.

She died on March 2, 1787, and is buried in old North Leith, near Edinburgh. There is a white Jacobite rose on her grave marker.

A word about the author…

Cynthia Breeding lives on the Gulf Coast of Texas with a very non-spoiled poodle-mix and enjoys walking and horseback-riding on the beach, as well as sailing.

www.cynthiabreeding.com